GW01086734

Full of Sin

Karl Vadaszffy

A Wild Wolf Publication

Published by Wild Wolf Publishing in 2009

Copyright © 2009 Karl Vadaszffy

All rights reserved. No part of this book may be reproduced, stored in a retrieval system or transmitted in any form or by any means without the prior written permission of the publishers, except by a reviewer who may quote brief passages in a review to be printed by a newspaper, magazine or journal.

First print

All Characters appearing in this work are fictitious. Any resemblance to real persons, living or dead, is purely coincidental.

ISBN: 978-0-9563733-0-4

Acknowledgement

With heartfelt thanks to Wiola, for encouraging me to stay positive; to my entire family; to Peter, for the fantastic cover design; to Sophie Hannah, for your guidance; to Wild Wolf, for embracing the dark side of fiction; and Dad – I hope you can see this.

'*The earth seemed unearthly. We are accustomed to look upon the shackled form of a conquered monster, but there – there you could look at a thing monstrous and free. It was unearthly, and the men were – No, they were not inhuman.*'

~ Joseph Conrad, *Heart of Darkness*

Today

If to sin means to do the unspeakable, the unthinkable, and to be willing to hurt, to want and therefore to take, to damn the consequences and seek personal gratification, gratification of all the senses, regardless of who you take down on the way, regardless of the pain you inflict, the destruction you cause, then I was a champion sinner because for me sinning was as normal as the sun rising and setting and while some of you may say it was sick I can't possibly comment; I'm not to judge; I can only say that I was so much a part of it – the actor in the central role, the one on whom everyone has an eye, the one in the spotlight; a spotlight that many crave, that few achieve, but that I grabbed, took and thrived in, until the day it all became too much, the day that my immoral soul took a step too far, had been consumed by all things sin for too long, began to choke, was desperate to surface for breath and couldn't live on in any other way than a way that was different, better, even purer. In only twenty-two years I've seen so much and done too much; sights that give people nightmares and acts that sicken the strongest of stomachs. The average person couldn't understand what I was because we couldn't be more different, for there came days when I knew nothing else – just sick old sin – and I loved every minute of it.

I can't escape the memory of the evening when I watched her tumble down the stairs. It's a vision that will never leave me. How her body flopped as it rolled towards the ground then stiffened up the moment before impact, as if she knew what was coming but could only brace for the collision. All this time later I can hear her mass as it bounced off the steps; I can hear her cries as she was carried through the air; and I can hear the crash as she landed at the bottom. At that moment I didn't know what to do, for acting violently had become alien, something to which I hadn't succumbed for almost three years – but I'd thrown her down the stairs and was smiling. The thing is, when I was violent I thrived on the power I felt; I loved being in control of another person; to know they were merely weak. And here I immediately felt it rearing its ugly head again.

Again.

I tower fifteen feet above my victim. Another to add to the long line that lies before it. It takes me a moment to process what I've done: Jodie is my victim. She's stretched out on her back, her hips are turned to the left and her legs are pressed against the wall. She mouths several groaning noises – not of pleasure, but of pain and suffering. I know I've caused the pain but it doesn't bother me. I don't care for Jodie and the hurt she must be experiencing; I only like what she gives me, and now my one regret is that I'll never get it from her again.

She gives it so good that it's the only thing on my mind. For one week we've repeated the first night. Alone in the house, I was reading. My makeshift parents were at dinner with friends. Jodie was out doing what she did best, apart from blowing: partying. *The Comfort of Strangers* was in my hands. Ian McEwan. Strange, indeed, how those you think you know can surprise you; how people with whom you are comfortable are actually sometimes the people you should fear the most. Sexy too.

As I turned a page, the front door banged shut and I heard feet shuffling downstairs. I pictured Jodie trying to remove her lace-up boots, the black leather tight on her skin, as she stumbled against the wall. I'd seen it happen many times before. Watched her, in fact.

Footsteps hit the stairs and made their way in my direction. She was moving slowly. I listened, the book no longer of interest. A dull thud. Some giggling. A cough. My name. "Oh Sean," sing-songy. More laughter and I got up to see what was going on.

She was a state, just like the previous time when she stumbled in from a night on the piss. The same as always. Pathetic but I liked it. With her right leg two steps higher,

6

revealing her toned upper thigh, Jodie was leaning against the wall and staring up at me.

"Hey, lover boy," she said, still laughing.

"Are you okay?"

No matter how she felt, she looked more than okay. She wore a low-cut black top, which showed the shape of her breasts and came to an end an inch above a pierced navel. I couldn't look at it but could look at her all day. A black skirt that rode high and black stockings covered the lower half of her body invitingly. Her legs looked incredible and my breathing instantly sped up and deepened. A few holes had amassed in her stockings. She spread her arms back behind her and licked her lips, her breasts pushing out. My desire grew and I wasn't going to hide it anymore.

"Help me up," she said.

I wanted her.

I went down a few steps towards her. The navel ring shone in the light of the lamp above our heads. I lifted my eyes and focused on her breasts. She saw where my gaze was fixed and she knew. Her long brown hair, which she'd curled today, stuck to her forehead and cheeks. I wanted to pull at it with my mouth.

"Put your arms around me," she said.

I obeyed. With my arm around her waist I helped her on and up. I thought she was letting me in.

One step up, she stumbled forwards and put her hand onto my leg for balance. Right then she saw it clear as could be.

"And what's this?" she said, running her fingers across my groin, feeling my stiffness. The ecstasy that tunnelled through my body made me quiver and I leaned back against the banister.

"Oops," she giggled, and I closed my eyes. That was when I heard and felt my zipper being undone. Her fingers crept their way inside my boxer shorts, the two buttons opening with ease. All the while, she sniggered. I came out in her hand like a jack-in-the-box and felt her finger nails gently moving over my length.

I leaned forwards and ran my hand down the small of her back, found a way underneath her skirt and onto her backside.

"Grab it," she said, releasing me. She rose to her feet and kissed me hard on the mouth as I squeezed.

She led me onto the landing. I fell into my bedroom door with her clinging to my lips. Kicking through the bedroom door and closing it behind her, she pushed me onto the bed and leapt on top as I fell. We rocked up and down on the springs. Her body rubbed against mine. She lifted my t-shirt off. Her tongue slid around my chest, searching for something. She found my belly button and spat in it.

I sat up, lifting her. My hand slid under her skirt and I pushed hard. In response her nails scratched down my chest. I bellowed and came alive.

She was totally up for it and took me on a ride I never thought I'd get on. Yes, I'd thought about her hot body on many a lonely night. Many times I'd thought about what I'd do to her if I ever got the chance. And within fifteen minutes I was completing the fantasy, kneeling above Jodie as she lay before me, her hands pressing her tits together, then spewing all over the place. It was the kind of pleasure you can't imagine, no matter how much you fantasise. And the beauty of it – it would happen again.

Indeed it has for the past week. I'm in my room and there's a quiet knock on the door. No one enters but I know what to do. I open up and peer down the landing. And each time the same sight lies in wait. There she is, standing in her bedroom doorway, wearing nothing but a bra and thong. Always black or red. One time with suspenders. And like a dog on heat I make my way to her, following her scent and that alluring *come to me*.

It's been a week of perfect fucking. But today, the seventh day, the knock hasn't come. I wait and wait, willing it, but nothing. We're alone in the house, so I can't see what's holding her up. I'm thinking about it so much I'm hard, so I decide to take the lead. I approach her bedroom, anticipating and fantasising about what I believe will happen, but I'm forced to pause outside the door when I hear what sounds like sobbing coming from within. For a moment I rest my ear against the rap star poster that has replaced the door. Yes, it's sobbing. But this is me and I'm not looking for tears. I'm looking for a fuck – nothing more, nothing less – and I've got that for the past six days. And she has too. So what the fuck is her problem?

I knock and enter when I hear a stifled "Come in." I close the door behind me. Whenever I stand in this room, my eyes have to adjust to the interior. Variations of pink dominate: pink wallpaper; pink fluffy carpet; a pink bed cover; pink bears propped on top of it. But Jodie's as opposite to pink as any girl can be. She's trouble; that's part of the attraction. She's involved with the wrong people, she does wild things, but she keeps the truth well hidden from her parents. There are times when she even seems as sneaky as me.

I stand there trying to work out the best way to ensure I get what I want. Jodie asks me to sit. I do as she requests, still expecting to get it. She talks at me for a time, fighting back tears, I can see. What we've done, she says, is nothing special and a mistake. Silently, I shake my head. It's my pleasure and she's demeaning it in this way. She doesn't regret it, she says – it was fun, but that's all. Fun we need to continue right now. She couldn't bear it if her parents found out. Fuck them; what about what I want? "We're supposed to be a family," she keeps repeating, shaking her head.

A family? "But you want it," I tell her. She wants to get fucked.

"No," she answers. "I don't. I told you, not anymore."

I can't hear this – I'll hit her if she carries on much longer – and I know for sure I have to change her mind. I'm positive I can convince her that we both want the same thing. It's what *I* want. Nobody ever says no to me. But she won't listen, so stubborn, frankly shy and subdued for the first time in her fucking life. I'm not a talker – I don't have the patience – so I try to change her mind the only way I know how: I reach my hand under her skirt and push. Her reply – she slaps me; so hard I fall back.

Deep inside, I feel something return.

9

I smile at her, lean forwards and return my hand to her leg, further up this time, harder. She squeals, lifting her left knee high in the air. It breaks the grip I have on her, knocks my arm out of the way and hits me on the chin. I writhe momentarily in pain, my mouth suddenly bloody, and that's all it takes.

Bitch! I'm ready to kill her. I'm enraged and an old friend is re-awoken. I lunge forwards, grab her by the shoulders and shake her around. She manages to knee me in the groin; I guess I'm out of practice. I fall to my knees and she runs from the room, but the smile hasn't vanished from my face. Just like old times.

I scramble to my feet, with blood dripping from my mouth onto the cream carpet, and go after her. I catch hold of her just as she begins to descend the staircase, pull her up so that she's standing level with me and press her up against the wall. She pushes, screams and throws her arms around, unable to connect another blow. Holding her to the wall with my left forearm against her throat, I plant my lips on hers, push with such force that I almost go through her face, and lift her top up with my other hand. In one very slow movement I get hold of her grotesque navel ring. The feel of it angers me further. I pull at it, savouring each moment. As the skin stretches, she bellows a guffaw of pain. I remember the sound well; remember how much I liked it before, when these things were commonplace. She knows what's coming. I place my tongue on hers as she cries. She begins to swing relentlessly, so I toy with her no more.

I come away from the parting kiss and ensure that our eyes are locked. Then I wrench at her hideous ring until it tears off. As metal and flesh part, she explodes with the most desperate cry I've ever heard. Blood rains from her midriff onto the carpet and wall. It covers my hands, warming me. Noticing the blood all over my fingers, I lick my lips and grin. She tries to shake free but still to no avail. I won't back off. Not until it's done.

She's sobbing and all I want to do is look at her. The sight of the whites of my eyes makes her cower further into the wall. I almost laugh at the sight of her, so pathetic she appears to be.

This is Jodie.

With my right hand I grab hold of her skirt. My fingers enter and rub against her pubic hairs. They're short and sharp, and memories of the past week of touching, pressing and licking her come back to me. I can feel myself getting hard again. Then I press my fingers deeper into her skin, consumed by the sensation that the touch arouses in me. My eyes close and I sigh.

As quickly as it came, the sensation evaporates, and in one swift motion, holding tightly onto her skirt and allowing our skin to disconnect, I spin myself around, forcing her whole body to follow. In a second I'm watching her tumble down the staircase. She flops, stiffens, collides. The thud, as her body connects with the carpet, echoes in my head.

Way above her I place my finger and the blood that covers it into my mouth, fall to my knees and hold my head in my other arm. Her sobbing tries to pierce through my consciousness but garners no response. Releasing my head, I look up to the Gods and breathe deeply through my nose. Then I stand up, the results of my attempted evening of pleasure before me, and feel satisfied in an altogether different way – one I'd not expected.

It's five or so minutes before I realise I've put myself back where it all began. That I've fallen again. I have to decide what to do – staying here isn't an option. I grab my wallet from my bedroom and pick up the pace as I go down the stairs, spitting the final remnants of blood onto the floor as I pass Jodie and her pain-ridden pleadings. In the kitchen I withdraw a series of bank notes from the drawer beneath the glasses' cabinet; spare money I know is hidden in the house in case of emergencies.

With the money in my pocket, my coat on my shoulders and a long stretch of my arms, I leave the kitchen, step over Jodie as she remains lodged on the floor and leave what has become my family for ever.

*

I've got nowhere to go, but right now I don't care. I've been alone before, dropped by everyone I've ever known, and I perfected how to wander the streets years ago.

It's been about an hour and I've come to an area of woodland not far from the place I recently called home. As I circle its grounds, images of what happened in the house tonight and over the past week flash in and around my consciousness. I see Jodie standing seductively in that doorway. I see my hand between her legs. I see her tongue draw over her lips. I see her hand taking me firmly. Then I see her body tumbling through the air. All of it – sexual or violent – in slow motion, my own film, one I direct and star in.

Oakley Park stands before me, metres away from the woods. It's empty. I approach the metal gate. It was painted black once, but the paint has peeled away and a dull grey dominates. Graffiti covers the gate posts, the perimeter fence and the solitary slide. Three years ago, when I arrived at the Andersons' home, Oakley Park was newly built and fresh. Now that freshness has dissipated and evolved into an eyesore.

I go in and sit astride a swing, rocking myself backwards and forwards. I lean my face against the metal chain that holds the seat in mid-air. Time to think about what to do and where to go. But I can't focus. My mind is fixed on the events of tonight and the evenings before. It makes the longing return, stronger than ever before. I begin to pace, so much is the tension circulating around my groin.

After ten minutes of not being able to get her body and what she's done to me out of my head, I creep underneath the slide, balance on my knees, careful not to cut myself further on any of the shards of glass that lie scattered all around me, and unzip my jeans. It's already hard as lead. My hand runs right up and down. Long, slow movements, my eyes shut the whole time. My cheeks and forehead tighten as the movements get sharper. So fast now I can feel it coming. Rising up as it does. And with Jodie and her body pounding away on top of me in my mind, it happens. I say her name aloud, almost a scream through gritted teeth, and feel released.

But despite the release and feeling the sensitivity of a burn victim, I still want more. She's all I can see. Her – that bitch. That bitch with the body I want to fuck.

Shaking my head to free it up and putting myself away, I decide that here is as good a place as any to spend the night. If the rains come I can stay right where I am, shelter beneath the slide. And I've got to think carefully. Fuck the thoughts of her and think. About what's next. About what's happened.

It doesn't take long before my thinking clears up. I ask myself, *Should I have done that?* And there's only one answer in my head: *Of course – you had to level the bitch*.

At that moment, I was alone again. I didn't feel worried yet, but I didn't know what to do. Somehow I'd have to rekindle the part of myself that knew how to survive – part of me that had lain dormant for so long. What had just happened wouldn't simply disappear and forget about me, so I knew I'd have to fight and fight hard.

Fifteen Years Ago

Blessings. Life in its purest form, long before corruption sets in. Entities to cherish, one could say. What else but children of course. As the years begin and gradually pass by, some of these beings are accepted and some are rejected as outcasts. A deck of cards collapses with more order. A child cannot determine which route – acceptance or rejection – judgmental society will choose for it. Problems arise for all kinds of reasons: it has the wrong social background; dislikeable parents; the wrong religion; the wrong skin colour; its nose is too big; it's too fat; it's shorter than it should be; it only has two arms – we've heard them all before. Then the child suffers. And the child becomes an adult who has suffered for too long.

Certainly a young child has no say in the matter of acceptance – a little boy or girl cannot comprehend the complexities between like and dislike, love and hate, right and wrong – so it falls upon the parent to fill the child with knowledge and guide it. But what if the parent fails the child? What if the parent is unable to distinguish between these himself? The child is left alone and helpless, that's what. It's here that rejection is at its fullest.

And it was at its fullest for Sean from the beginning. Rejection played a concrete part in his life from the outset.

He was born a mistake, the result of one of many drug-filled, alcohol-fuelled, paid-for romps.

Mary Monroe, known as Melinda by trade, was a hard-working, hard-pounding whore. She was also Sean's mother. From the age of fourteen, she was living on the streets. By the age of fifteen, a mere two months later, she was working on them.

She left home the subject of her father's nasty sexual appetite for too long. His wife wasn't enough for him; he'd pound on her and pound away at her, yet he still craved more.

Like the loneliest moon, Mary staggered through her time, alone, in fear, waiting for the next onslaught to begin. It happened at its worst near the end on a daily basis. Each time her mother just stood by watching, nursing her own wounds and never those of her daughter. Inadequate as a mother and as a human being.

The time that it had been going on felt endless. Mary frequently imagined ways out of this eternal hell. She had no friends to whom she could turn, but even if they were there she knew she wouldn't be able to tell. She vowed to remain silent about her torment forevermore. If she could ever become genuinely intimate with another human being – and she doubted she ever could – she'd never empower them by revealing her dirty, little secret. She'd keep it buried, for there would never be another day when she'd be the weaker sex.

Her determination stood fast until the day she discovered she was carrying Sean inside her. That day somehow man had beaten her again.

It was two months shy of her fifteenth birthday when Mary vowed that the secret of her trespassed innocence would die the day she died herself. One final time had Mary come home from school and allowed him to touch her there. And one final time had she watched her mother stand by as it happened. She'd stopped crying about it some time ago; she'd been turned into an empty vessel. She'd learned to simply stand there and take it.

On the night that her life started its nosedive into a deeper hell when instead it was supposed to take off to new, brighter horizons, Mary walked out of her bedroom, a tiny, ramshackle alcove, for the last time. She entered the lounge and looked at the television that was playing a late-night episode of Jerry Springer. Before the television set, she saw the drunken, sleeping forms of her parents' bodies, his head carelessly strewn across her lap, much like one road intersects with another. With two empty glasses by its side the gin bottle on the table had been polished off. Looking down at them, she didn't feel anything for her parents, not even hate which, too, had been sucked from her body screaming. But she wished that neither of them would wake up. Then she'd be rid of them for ever. If that would happen they'd only be lurking in the depths of her mind, they wouldn't be able to find her, and she'd learned about ways to numb painful memories. She'd learned from the best.

As she reached for the door handle which she hoped would be the key to her freedom, she kept her eyes on her parents, even though she knew they wouldn't wake up, and she shuddered – at the scene that lay before her eyes and at the prospect of what lay in her future.

She walked out of the door and left for ever.

*

Sorrow and uncertainty were what Mary encountered. She'd thought about leaving her parents many times in the past, but she'd not once thought about where she'd go, what she'd do and how she'd manage when the moment came.

With only a small amount of money in her jeans pocket, the streets were an unwelcoming place for Mary. She was in no way streetwise. She walked as fatigue set in, wondering whether she'd made the right choice, comparing the pain and discomfort she now felt with the turmoil she'd left behind.

Young, innocent and hungry, she simply didn't know which way to turn. She kept moving – had to keep warm – but without a destination in mind. She passed so many buildings that made her feel so small – lots of signs of life and all unaware of where she'd come from – but she no longer knew where she was, so far had she ventured. A wave of fear engulfed her whole body. She was consumed by the same kind of shake that used to overtake her when he approached with that look in his eyes.

By the side of the busy road on which she'd found herself she began to panic. Her lips trembled as the rain, snot-like, dripped from her chin, and her knees buckled. She fell hard, grazing both knees and drawing blood. Her eyes welled up and

16

she looked to the heavens. She let out her first scream in many years, one of absolute terror. The high-pitched scream elevated then tailed off into a series of sobs that subsided only for the occasional gasp for air.

Mary didn't notice the car as it pulled over at the side of the road. She wasn't aware of the sound of approaching footsteps; she was only aware of a strange presence when someone crouched beside her and placed a hand upon her shoulder.

A voice asked, "Are you all right?"

For a moment, Mary felt soothed by the question and the tone of the voice, until she realised the voice belonged to a man.

"Honey, are you all right?" it repeated. "Is everything okay?"

Without raising her eyes Mary inched backwards. All she could think was, My God, it's him. How did he find me so quickly? She didn't want to see into his eyes. With him she feared life itself, yet she knew she'd have to look up and meet his glare somehow. How could she bring herself to once again look into the eyes of the monster?

The growl demanded confirmation. "Listen, I asked you if you're all right." She knew she was in danger. "You look dreadful."

Despairing, she lashed her arms out towards him, connected with his arm – the stranger, the monster, her father – leapt to her feet and ran, ignoring the pain that soared from her knees.

"Hey!"

She ran along the path, small stones spraying into the air as she dragged her feet – her mother had always told her to stop dragging her feet. Walk properly, she'd say, the smell of liquor pouring from her breath. Lift your feet up properly.

Still in view of the man she believed to be her father, Mary spotted an opening in the hedge next to which she was running. She lunged through it, leaving him behind as he followed her only with his gaze, and she let out a scream of release and pain and fear from her lips as she disappeared from view.

Dumbfounded, the stranger – the one good-willed passer-by who was willing to offer help – returned to his car. As he opened the driver's side door, he exhaled deeply and thought, What the hell was that all about? He wondered why.

The answer was simple: he was a man.

*

Six hours later the tears had subsided, the blood had dried and night had begun to fall.

The first night away from home had been easier to handle than Mary had expected. She'd walked away from her parents at almost three o'clock in the morning and had got only a little way when daylight started to creep through. But now Mary was cold and unsure, and the prospect of being alone and vulnerable for ten hours of darkness frightened her. She wanted to find a busy area, an all-night café, a night club; anywhere so that she wouldn't be completely alone.

Finding life came eventually. By now she was almost penniless, having spent much of the new day warming her heart and mind with sweets, coffee and fast food. So now she'd suffer even more. Nonetheless, when the crowds dispersed, she yearned for other places full of people, not for food and drink, but for what they sucked in, held and then spat outside: life. Crowds meant Mary Monroe had to keep moving, for crowds didn't remain static for long.

In the depths of the second night, despite her best efforts, she couldn't find any more crowds. The darkness started to creep her out. As she walked along yet another dimly lit street, every out-of-place noise and each howl of the wind took her closer to the edge.

Despair.

She started to walk faster, but her mind raced with memories, unspeakable terrors; images of her father approaching and the chilling touch of his hand.

Before she knew it her pace had slacked. Her body shivered, yet she was sweating. As she felt ready to return to her

18

knees, through her tears she noticed a solitary figure in the distance, the first she'd seen in almost an hour, dressed sleekly in black and lit only by a streetlamp. Insecurely, Mary made her way to the lonely figure, only to see when she'd neared her target that the lonely figure was not so lonely. Buried in the shadows behind the woman, two others stood similarly dressed.

Mary stopped and stood at a cautious distance from them. She whispered hoarsely, "Excuse me."

None of them heard her or maybe they pretended not to.

She braced herself and tried again, this time a little louder. "Excuse me, can you help me?"

With a cursory turn of the head, the overdone yet attractive redhead looked in Mary's direction. Her eyebrows raised in a way that might have indicated surprise, annoyance or both. "Don't think about using my patch, honey," she warned.

Mary looked confused. "I need your help," she said. "I don't know what to do."

"Uh-ha, and how do you expect to attract anyone looking like that?" she asked, disapprovingly nodding her head towards Mary's clothes.

"Please help me," Mary continued as more tears began to break through. "I need your help. I'm lost."

"Aren't we all, honey?"

Cue in the other two women showing sympathy and playing the Samaritans, and that was how it all began – when the nightmare life was born and started to spiral out of control. It evolved as a miracle in disguise. Absolute disguise.

*

Long considered to be the oldest profession in history, prostitution was truly alive and Mary stumbled upon it and its alluring ways unexpectedly. Desperately needed easy money.

Their names – presumably their street names – were Denise (the redhead), Janet and Rita. Mary told them about herself, not everything of course, but they liked her. She, on the other hand, hated herself. They befriended her, showed her a new kind of life and introduced her to some possibilities.

For two evenings Mary stayed with them and felt safe, for one of them was always free. They looked after her, nurturing and treasuring the new blood, even though Mary had no idea about their plans for her. For now she saw them as friends and that meant the world to her.

On the second night, Mary was at her usual place, seated leaning against the wall, her eyes to the ground, her hands clasped around her tucked-in knees. A car pulled up, a cloud of smoke behind it – the fourth of the evening, of which only one had borne any fruit – and a sneering face popped out of the lowered window. Janet approached the driver first but swiftly returned to her starting position. Rita was next but she too had no luck, so it was left to Denise to work her magic. Mary had noticed how it was normally down to Denise to convince the punters to part with their hard-earned cash and she was usually successful.

Surprised, Mary realised that Denise had failed when she heard the voice from within the car say, "I want the one over there, the young one."

Mary raised her head shyly. Lowered it then raised it again, desperately.

As the three women turned towards their new competition, Mary fought to prevent herself from bursting into tears. Noticing the fear spread across Mary's face Denise said seductively, brushing against the car, "She's not for sale, honey, but me, I'll do anything you want."

To Mary's relief the man in the car changed his mind. Denise hopped in and the car sped off, leaving the other two women to nurse Mary from the shock of what had just happened. Denise had said to the others from the beginning that Mary wouldn't just jump at the opportunity; she'd take some time to come around – like they all do.

To a young girl like Mary all their discussions made the business sound glamorous, although she knew deep at heart that it wasn't. A few alluring words couldn't convince her that this place wasn't one step closer to hell. But it was also far away from the other hell she'd left behind and for that she was thankful.

As their time together featured more pep talks and attractive financial offers, Mary was drawn ever closer to the kind of life she'd never thought possible. Denise had taken Mary in and cared for her. Mary could talk to Denise and rely on her, but she knew even at this early stage that it couldn't last indefinitely. She'd have to look after herself one day, and how to do that was limited.

The greatest, most unexpected feat was that Mary thought very little of her parents. She felt more secure – an inkling of happiness because of her new life. At times she felt like she belonged with Denise, the kind of thought that had previously evaded her.

Then, finally, she was drawn in.

She hadn't thought of her father much but on that fateful night, two hours after dolling up and making her mind up, Mary – or Melinda as Denise chose to introduce her to her first client – was ready. Standing by the side of the road in the darkness and lit only by the towering streetlamp, Mary – Melinda – looked a picture in her black bra, see-through wrap and black leather jacket. Not much was left to the imagination. Down below she wore tanned stockings and a black skirt so short it rode up. Her shoulder-length dark hair and naïve green eyes exuded insecurity and looked out of place. At the tender age of fifteen, all the tenderness and innocence of youth had been beaten out of her years ago, and tonight, as her first car, client and pay cheque approached, that beating would continue.

As the passenger door drew open and revealed nothing but a dark tube, Denise beckoned Melinda in, and Mary heard only one thing: her father's voice, as the stranger in the car announced, "Nice."

As Melinda got into the car, the three women looked on, pleased with themselves. As their smiles beamed, the car pulled away, leaving nothing behind but polluting smoke, consensual virginity on its way out and the prospect of yet more painful memories in its wake.

Later Today

The rains came heavily the night I ran from the Andersons. I knelt beneath the slide, sheltering from the onslaught of rain, and went through what had happened until my legs went to sleep and forced me to stand up. As I straightened my back and the adrenaline wore off, the pain from banging my head on the staircase returned. It dug in and thrived on the discomfort it caused. I placed the palm of my hand on the back of my head, somehow imagining that my touch was magical and would simply wish the pain away. As the rain fell upon me and dripped down my face, I closed my eyes. My mind continued to race even though my body was shutting down from fatigue. I still saw Jodie in my mind's eye. I saw her curves, and I still wanted more. I saw her smile, and I heard her scream. I saw her tears, and I couldn't care less. I saw her skin, and I saw flesh tear. I saw rejection in her eyes, and I felt angry. Desperately alone now, I only felt angry. Scared would creep up on me later.

Darkness continued to fall and so did my body. Such acts as those in which I partook take their toll. So I returned to my shelter, my home for now, when I'd endured enough rain. Once again I crouched down, but the tingling soon came back to my knees. I swallowed what little pride I had left and slouched on the ground. I sat there among crushed beer cans, sharp to the touch, and sticky drink bottles. Litter and alcohol sick riddled the place like a puzzle. I even saw a syringe. This used to be a place for kids; I used to hang out here when I first arrived, when I was young, my moments alone when they were granted to me, before it was overrun by pure filth. I felt sick. It and I had come to this.

This.

Look at you. Living in this shit. Pathetic. You are pathetic. And why? All because of some slag who gave you

22

nothing. Even more pathetic. You couldn't even get laid when she was begging for it before. She started it last week. She came to you. She wanted you. She wanted to get fucked. So who's to blame? If she'd have acted like every day of the past week none of this would've happened. I'd still be there, happy, warm. We'd be resting together now, tired, out of breath, naked and naked. So whose fault is it you're here? The one who pouted and posed and possessed you, that's who. That bitch.

The anger in my blood rises ten degrees. I want to punch someone. Something. I search the area for anything I can get hold of.

My gaze stops as it falls upon the swings and the plastic seats that belong to them. I leap to my feet. I can't control myself. I get to the swings and lift one of the seats high into the air. I bring my right fist towards it, using all the weight behind my shoulder to push. Water sprays from it as my hand connects with a snap and the swing seat flies and collides with the metal frame from which it hangs. For a moment I feel nothing except a rage burning out of control deep within. Then a numbness, and an almighty throbbing overcomes my hand. Despite the pain, the fires churn away at me and I kick at the ground. I kick the swing frame and I scream. Again and again I bring my foot crashing against the metal. I don't feel the rain as it soaks me and I can't hear my screams. My eyes well up and I fall to the ground, clutching my head. My mind thinks of only one thing. My life: this is my life. What the hell am I supposed to do?

I was going to fight and fight hard. Only I didn't know it yet. I lay on the litter-strewn play-safe tarmac, a beaten, wretched soul. I closed my eyes and hoped the world would disappear. I hoped it would vanish and suck me away to a distant place with it.

*

I awoke the next morning to the sound of a double act of dogs barking. I squinted through my eyelids and tasted that early morning taste. Usually I liked it, but today I wished it would leave me alone. I was back under the slide, but I couldn't remember returning there the night before. I lay on the ground among leaves and stones. My neck hurt. The daylight was too bright for my eyes. As I moved onto my side, a sudden sharp pain radiated all over my foot. How I regretted those kicks. My clothes were dry, but I felt soaked. By what I couldn't tell yet. I reached for the back of my head to check on the second source of pain I felt and found a small lump. A reminder of those stairs and Jodie, as if I needed one.

I sat up, stretched my back and tried to look over the fence. No success, but I heard two voices approaching. I crept on the balls of my feet, crouching on my knees – I didn't want anyone to see me, not like this and not after what had happened. Oakley Park isn't far from the Andersons' home. It could've been anyone who'd recognise me. I'd no idea who knew about Jodie and me, so I feared detection – I'd committed a crime after all – and in no way did I want confrontation. Not with so much pain coming from my body.

When the voices were close by, I edged to the far side of the slide and climbed onto it. There I was sheltered from my potential observers by the slide's peak. I glimpsed around the side and saw a man and woman, probably in their mid-twenties, in deep conversation. As they spoke, they held hands and looked at each other in a way I couldn't identify. With them, two dogs – one black; the second white – played joyfully. They barked, bounced off each other, sniffed for a second, then barked again. Such simple enjoyment. As the man said something, the woman laughed. The man smiled too and pressed the back of his hand against the woman's cheek. Her skin must have felt so smooth, so soft to touch. His other hand squeezed hers tightly. He pulled her close and kissed her lips. When he released her, she smiled again, as did he. And it was opposite a smile such as this that I suddenly craved to be. It was odd. They looked so happy and content and I thought I deserved to feel like that too. Then I experienced something extraordinary: a gnawing in my stomach. A tightening. Strange. Uncomfortable. Like someone had fought a way inside and was tying strings of me. Suddenly the sight of Jodie's naked body made me wince. I couldn't watch anymore; I had to get out of there.

I moved off the slide and ran. Ran like hell. Without glancing back I barged through the gate. The couple had probably seen me by now, either to identify me or wonder what the hell I was doing, but I didn't care. I wasn't stopping for anyone or anything. I ran towards a group of trees and entered the forest. I leapt behind the first big tree I spotted, dropped against the bark out of sight and closed my eyes. My hands clawed at the tree trunk like I feared it too would abandon me.

I'd just witnessed, and reacted to in a way alien to me, what I feared I'd never have myself: love. I guessed.

I moved my back up and down the bark. At first, comforting, relieving an itch. But I didn't stop. Moving quicker, I pushed harder and it gnawed at my skin. I knew blood had been drawn. The pain brought me to tears but I didn't stop. I couldn't. I had to be punished. I wanted to die.

Scared set in now. Really set in.

*

I was on the streets for almost three weeks, abandoned I believed at the time by the Andersons and everyone else. Why do people never forgive? Why do they always give up on you?

It was difficult for the first few hours of the second day, but something happened to energise me. After I ran back into the woods and thought about the couple I'd seen, about what it made me desire, I headed deeper in, further than any time I'd gone to clear my head in the past. With the pain from my head and foot now overrun by the fresh agony caused by my back, I waded through the mud for quite some time, stepping over twigs and nettles, listening to the annoying rustling all around me as I disturbed this animal and that. I pushed myself in between the overgrown and the destroyed, making a route by force if one wasn't already there. I cut my fingers and wrists, scratched my forehead and got stung, so much so that my legs even itched beneath my trousers. I wanted to scream at the frustration I felt but did all I could to bear it. The deeper I got, the further I travelled and the more obstructions I encountered, the more there was that got in my way. Aside from the frustration that was dwelling in my gut, I was confused and prayed to find a way out. The only consolation came from knowing that I would find myself a long way from where I started, which would make any search for me difficult.

I must have been clawing my way along for three hours before I heard the noise of traffic. And it sounded, for the first time, glorious. On an average day, glorious would be an inappropriate word, but today the traffic chimed in my ears like the most beautiful symphony. Before, I'd started to panic, doubting I'd ever find a way out. The mind's a dangerous thing, like a weapon sometimes, only the wounds from it were self-inflicted in my case. I couldn't bear the thought of spending a night alone. *Not here.* But traffic meant I was close to somewhere I could call my destination, so the panic began to seep away.

Streams of brighter light emerged between a mass of trees in the distance. To say I was relieved would be an understatement. What I'd do when I emerged I didn't know.

When I sprang out from the woods, I felt like a newborn seeing its first glimmer of daylight, while a ray of sunshine blocked my path and forced my eyes to squint. It was a welcoming sight, I can tell you; a new beginning of sorts. I found myself at the side of a main road. Car after car passed by me, each driver totally oblivious to my predicament, unaware of why I was there, from where I'd come and indeed to where I was going. I, too, was ignorant when it came to that. *If only they knew*, I thought.

Opposite me was a line of trees, symmetrical to those behind me. Behind them more woodland. No way was I getting into that again. To my right a steep hill formed, carrying the road and trees with it. All I could see up to its peak was trees. I imagined this sight on a bright summer's day. People must come here to relax. People must cycle and dog walk in the woods. Fun with sex too. My mind took over and I was picturing the summer sunshine. I imagined some fields nearby and hundreds of hopeful sunbathers baring their chests, desperate for the sun to develop those bronzed and red looks. Bustling with life, it'd be. Only now, as I stood here, the ground shone with rain residue and the sun looked threatened by the intimidating clouds that were moving in. I had to make a decision and move. To my left, the road was flat but arced off into a sharp bend about half a mile away. I couldn't see further and had no idea what lay beyond it. Standing in the middle of two choices, I had no idea which to take.

Simply to find a way out I took the road to the left. I'd faced a lot in my life, but the prospect of this – of not knowing what the hell to do and where the hell I was – made me feel too young and powerless. I hated feeling like this; everyone does. I'd taken off from the Andersons without a moment's thought about ramifications of my actions. I believed I'd just walk away from one house and somehow straight into another. But who on earth would house an uncontrollable monster? Isn't that what I was? Besides, I didn't realise, until I had the spare hours during which to think about what had happened, that it was I who'd chosen to be homeless. So who could help me now? And who'd give a second's thought to helping me once they found out about me? Someone my age has a lot of explaining to do if they suddenly appear from nowhere. Like a magic trick. Or like a magic trick gone wrong in my case.

If I'd have stayed with Jodie to face the music, I'd no doubt have been carted off again – and I didn't want that like most people don't want a fatal accident – but would that have been better than this, than being alone, than being nothing? Anderson, though – he could be a nut. I didn't want to face him. Words can't even describe how crazy he could be. One time, Jodie and I were with him in his car when another driver cut in front of us. Instead of flashing his lights at the guy or mumbling – even screaming – profanities, Anderson followed him, flashing his lights and screaming profanities. When we stopped at a red light a few miles further on, he got out of the car and charged towards the other driver. The guy saw him coming and tried to get out of his car to face Anderson. He didn't make it. Anderson caught him with three right hands as he was half in, half out of his car. Then he just got back into our car and drove us home. Whistling. Just like that. I think he viewed it all as a game and he loved playing it. You should've seen the twisted smile on his face and the gleam in his eyes. Jodie was petrified. As soon as the car pulled to a stop, she ran from the car and locked herself in her room. Anderson turned to me when she was gone and nodded. Then he held his finger over his lips, making sure I understood to keep what had happened quiet, and he walked away. Still smiling of course. I've never forgotten it. The sight of that finger covering those lips.

As I recount what was going through my mind at the time, you might ask me, what about Jodie? The truth is I reacted selfishly. When I ran away, I thought only of myself. I even blamed her. I didn't once think about the huddled mass I'd left lying at the bottom of the staircase in the Anderson house. I didn't once think, *Boy, I hope Jodie's all right.* In absolute honesty, I didn't care. I felt nothing for her but a longing in the loins – and anger. Now, of course, I regret my actions. But it took time to get me this far. I was lost. The name Jodie only returned to my mind the day after I found my way to new shelter. When I dreamt of her, and of her body. Only it was cold and lifeless, and I derived no pleasure from the dream, only more pain.

Still free of such thoughts, I followed the same road for what seemed like an age. The trees, so many of them, followed me along the road and made me feel trapped in a maze.

Eventually I lost track of time, but after several hours I came across a petrol station from which I picked up a sandwich and drink. Thirst and hunger had overtaken me, quicker than any of the many cars passing by.

"How far's the nearest town?" I asked the assistant.

He had a thin, pointed nose and wispy brown hair. His appearance made him seem years older than he probably was.

"You're in it," he answered, speaking through his nose rather than his mouth. I struggled to distinguish his words from the buzzing that escaped his lips. "Keep on up the road there –" he pointed a bony finger to the left – "and you'll start hitting more life fairly soon."

I nodded and headed off. Outside it had finally started to rain. I cursed and lifted the collar of my coat up to protect my neck. Realising it wouldn't help, I thought, *What the hell*, and made my way onwards.

I reached the centre of nothing more than a small village after twenty minutes. On my left side the road branched off to make space for a row of shops: the customary newsagent; a florist with a colourful, albeit unattractive, insignia displayed high above the window; and a couple of others selling all you could dream of, begging the locals to come here and not the huge supermarket with cheaper prices only minutes away. On the other side of the road three houses, all made of white stone, rather dirty and with thatched roofs, backed onto a field. A path next to them invited you to go further, behind a small wall and round behind some bushes. It probably led to a green haven, full of bright flowers and the smell of dew. I didn't dare go there. I drew my gaze back to the houses and observed how easily they could burn – after all, they looked covered in grass. There was a hedgerow that lined the front of the three houses and before it several shiny new cars were parked. They spat out and ate up the word *rich*. If there were any other houses, I couldn't see them. They were probably sheltered from the wrong kinds and the owners were probably off playing golf somewhere hot.

Beyond the final shop, a hairdressing salon empty of customers, I caught sight of a sign. I decided to check it out, wanting to find a comfortable shelter for the impending night's sleep. Or attempt to sleep. I started to pass the salon. A brunette inside was looking into a mirror fixing her make-up. She caught my attention and I stopped. Her right hand was plying away at her eyelashes. I can still see that hand working. I wondered if she liked what she saw. I did. She was wearing the standard hairdressing rack: a black long-sleeve top and black jeans. Her shoes, too, were black and had flat soles. I saw how tight her rear appeared to be in those jeans. Maybe I salivated. I leant towards the window, rested my forehead on it and suddenly wanted more. I thought about how her body would feel to touch and how it would feel to push inside her. Frustration at not getting what I wanted yesterday set in again. I could almost hear Jodie's moans when the woman in the shop turned around and faced me. When she saw me – and how pathetic I must've looked, my tongue hanging out or something equally ridiculous – she giggled. I didn't like that. I turned my head; she'd embarrassed me. I quickly slid out of view around the side of the building.

Welcome to the park. It was certainly labelled appropriately, much more of a park than Oakley Park. There were so many attractions. Swings of all sizes sat in wait. There were three see-saws arranged in order of height and a roundabout – it looked like it could hold a dozen kids. Rounding off the list were five horse-shaped springboards, all made of brightly painted wood, a large sandpit, currently waterlogged and empty of buckets and spades, and a climbing frame painted in the colours of the rainbow. I wondered if that meant I'd find the fictional pot of gold nearby. Behind a metal gateway, a paddling pool drained of water awaited the summertime and the splashers and bathers that come hand in hand with it. A freshly painted wooden fence surrounded the whole complex, keeping the kids safe, but there were no children visible today – rain scares easily. By the side of the park were several benches, standing opposite a huge field on which picnic tables waited to serve the summer crowds.

My heart froze momentarily when I glanced further ahead and my eyes came to a halt on the sixth bench along. Two guys were slouched upon it with a girl lying across their laps. Her legs were draped over the armrest. Next to them, three other guys were on the ground. Two leant back on their elbows; the other was stretched out on his stomach. Another girl, a cute blonde, sat astride his backside. Seeing the two of them, my longing for the female touch drove at me harder. They were laughing and drinking from a plastic bottle that was being passed around. I could guess what they were drinking and alcohol and a group of desperate-to-impress guys are a bad mix. I didn't want them to notice me, but I needed to check the park out. To do that meant

30

passing them. I contemplated turning away to avoid the possibility of confrontation – but when I noticed a small building in the distance, I couldn't give up because my need for shelter was too dominant. The building looked like some kind of hut, abandoned perhaps – its windows were boarded up. Filth covered its outside; it looked very much out of place as, indeed, did I. I couldn't see anything else, but the prospect of a roof under which to shelter appealed more than the possible threat that lay in wait.

I decided to go for it. I took several steps onto the grass in an attempt to distance myself from the group. I walked at a steady pace in an attempt to appear confident, but inside I started quaking. Keeping my head low, I tried to wish time away as I moved on, some ten or fifteen feet between us now, but all clocks had frozen. I thought about what I'd do if I were in the group, eager to impress a girl and my friends – I'd never had the chance, but I thought about it nonetheless – if I saw a dirty, solitary figure walking by. That's right, they did what I would've done too if I were fortunate enough to have been one of them.

"Hey, pig," one of them on the bench called out. I didn't know which one because I wouldn't look at them. *Maybe that'll make it better.* "Ain't no sty around here, mate," the same barely-broken voice yelled.

The others laughed. I could feel my face redden, but I pushed on through yet more embarrassment and the infernal rage building up within. Besides, I was passing them now. *Just keep on. You'll be out of the way soon.*

"What a skank," I heard another male voice say.

"You know what they say about the dirty ones," the cowgirl said. "Really wild in the sack." I caught sight of her out of the corner of my eye. When she noticed my glance, she started to ride the guy underneath her, grinding her hips back and forth. I couldn't believe what she was doing. She made several groaning noises for effect and he did too, encouraged by her. "Baby" came from his mouth. The others roared hysterically. And that was when I made my mistake. As soon as I did it, I knew I'd live to regret it. I hesitated, only for a split second, and I looked further round to them. I tried to continue, but my mind raced. Before I could acknowledge to myself that they were bound to react and before I could tell myself to act as though nothing had happened, the guy under the girl noticed my hesitation. It was his time to act now; he had to. He pushed the girl aside like the piece of garbage she was.

"You," he called at me as he got up. I just kept on moving and quickened my pace. "Hey, I'm talking to you, you little pig," he shouted again. He made a snorting noise. The others responded accordingly to his wonderful wit. He didn't stop there. "You. Pigboy." More approving gasps of laughter filled the brisk air and I refused to stop moving. "You looking at my girl?" he carried on. "How the fuck dare you!"

I wanted out of there. *Not now, not here, not this, don't*, I kept thinking. *I just want to find somewhere to kip.* I didn't want to fight; my body hurt too much. Plus he had a group of inept friends to back him up. But just because they were inept, that didn't mean they'd have difficulty taking me on. Me, I was alone. One person can only do so much. *Keep moving.*

He trotted to catch up with me and, when he was within feet of me, he moved forwards exaggeratedly, but only a little distance in reality. I couldn't see him in my peripheral vision anymore, but his footsteps stopped. I continued moving, creating more space between us. He kept calling me, but his words were merely a blur. I stayed focused on my objective: get to the hut.

I was nearing the hut when I heard it.

"How the fuck dare you, you homo."

Homo.

"You wanna watch me fuck?"

The words ring in my ears. So loud is his voice that I want to place my hands over them to stop the drilling. I freeze dead in my tracks and glare at the ground. He's pissed me off now and I know I'm going to lose control. My body starts to shake and I know I'm back. I turn on my toes and stare the guy right in the eyes. I stand completely still, unaware of anything around me. All I see is his eyes. He hesitates at the sight of me just long enough to let me know I have the advantage, but then he remembers why he's doing this and snaps out of it. He's fooling no one.

Those behind him call out, egging him on, desperate to see a fight, and I almost laugh at how pathetic they seem. Motherfucker's going to get it. I hear one of the guys shout, "Go on," and the twat opposite me stomps in my direction. I almost laugh at his flat-footed movements.

As he reaches the final few metres, he tries to sound fearless. It isn't working. "You squaring up to me?" he asks and all I can do is look into his weedy eyes. He's blinking incessantly.

He arrives on my doorstep and places his shoulders opposite my shoulders, his nose opposite my nose. I don't answer him. He's a worm of a boy, a fucking piss ant, perhaps marginally older than me, but far less anything else, a peasant in all reality. His face is scrunched up and his nose looks like it belongs to a rat or at least has been chewed by one. His head is shaved and he wears an earring on his right ear. I hate that. Earrings on men make me sick. This prick makes me sick. He's far skinnier than his face suggests and plenty shorter than me, so much so that I'm looking down the bridge of his nose, almost the perfect angle to spit on it.

He tries again. "Arsehole, you trying to square –"

I don't let him finish the sentence. My jaw clamps down on his nose as it loiters too near my face. I bite hard and he reduces in size, squeaking and squealing. His legs begin to give way, but I don't let go, so he's left hanging there. I hear his friends shouting from afar and see them start running towards us from the corner of my eye. *It'll soon be time to back off.* I take hold of his neck and squeeze hard, my teeth still firmly fixed on his nose. He gasps and a few more pathetic cries escape his mouth. I open my mouth, pull his head back and look him square in the eyes. Deeper still. Bug-eyed, he is, like he's met an immortal.

"Yeah," I whisper. "I guess I am squaring up to you."

Tears stream from his eyes. A drop falls onto my arm. My gaze follows it and, seeing this, so does his. He looks back at

33

me, his eyes begging to be set free. Full-on fear; I love it. *Closer, they're getting closer. Get ready.*

Our eyes are locked again. I nod my head. He shakes his, his eyes clenching shut.

His friends are too close for comfort, so I release his neck and take hold of the sides of his head with my fingernails. With one swift movement, I drag my fingers down both sides of his face, taking clumps of his skin with me to add to the grime already under my nails. A wave of air, which I feel press against my chin, releases from his lungs. I lift my knee as sharply as I can, deep into his stomach. As he falls towards the ground, I kick him in the mouth.

Yes, we're square.

I ran. I was sensible. I knew couldn't face that many guys. I understood my limitations when it came to fighting. I ran to the white hut and beyond it. I kept running and didn't stop until I was free from those pursing me.

But that boy had strangely energised me. I'd been reawakened. Despite where I was at that precise moment, my confidence started to rekindle. I had courage and I definitely had strength enough over him. Perhaps, just perhaps, somehow I'd be all right.

*

The adrenaline was running too freely, right through me like a man on speed. I was in a McDonald's wolfing down a burger and fries, guzzling a coke, and my body was shaking. Too fast, I choked.

I'd acted without thought in the park. I'd shown them what I was capable of and I'd protected myself. And I'd won. Seeing the cowgirl and the guy had brought back memories of pleasure that I wanted to experience again. And beating the hell out of that guy had brought back memories of my past, lain dormant for so long, so I craved to feel that power again.

After I swallowed a final piece of nothing more than distilled skin that's commonly accepted as a meal, I deposited my waste in the rubbish bin, as requested. After eating that food, I could very well have jumped in myself. I took note of the disturbed faces of everyone I passed when they saw the state I was in, so I went into the bathroom to clean up a little. I washed my face, scrubbing, really scrubbing, at the grime that had built up so quickly and plentifully. My wet hands brushed through my hair several times. I almost felt refreshed. Finally, my face gave the appearance of moderate cleanliness, but I knew I'd soon need to do something less temporary.

I left the so-called restaurant and crossed the road. A lady held the door open for me as I entered the pharmacy that was across the street. I smiled my acknowledgement to her, but I doubted she could see it through her rocket-launcher-length bifocals. I ran my eyes across the aisle contents markers that hung from the ceiling. An almighty task to search three whole aisles for something.

I found my way around the maze of shelving and grabbed a can of deodorant from a shelf – aisle two, left-hand side, unit two, third shelf down, in case you were wondering. I took the lid off and sprayed all over myself, on top of and underneath my shirt, as I walked towards the cashier. The woman standing behind the counter was old, I mean old like why-the-hell-are-you-working-instead-of-spending-the-last-of-your-days-lying-resplendently-in-some-retirement-village-being-waited-on-hand-and-foot?-old. She wore a green overall and white jacket, kind of like lab technician garb, both of which complimented her white, frizzy mop nicely. She looked like she'd been stuck in one of those hairdresser blow dry machines for hours; either that or she'd discovered static before Einstein. Her skin was loose, so much so that her nose was lost somewhere between her three chins. She, too, wore glasses the size of long-range binoculars. I offered her an incredibly fake smile and she frowned at me as I handed her the deodorant can and some cash. I don't know why I didn't just lift the bloody thing. She was hardly in a state to chase after me, much less see what I was doing at such a distance. I didn't hand her the cash; I placed it on the counter Eastern European style, and she didn't hand me my change either. Lifting the coins up, I flicked one into the air, caught it and was on my way. As I turned and began to walk to the exit, I swore I heard her *tsk*. That made me stop. To respond I remained still then moved the deodorant can to my backside. I bent forwards so that I could touch the floor with my other hand, sprayed the contents of the can onto my arse and left, shock spread widely across her cretin face, a smile on mine as I peered back.

Outside I removed all the money I had in my pockets and began to count it as I walked, destination unknown. While I counted, even though the Anderson trust fund had helped me out, I knew the reasonable amount I had left wouldn't last long. I'd never funded any kind of lifestyle before, even one as stone-age as this, but I knew I had to be careful.

Eyeing up the scenery, I walked around for a time. A lot of what I saw, mostly female, caught my attention and most definitely met with my approval. This place, small as it was, was full of testosterone-grabbing, hormone-sucking girls and women. While I felt I was in an early heaven, the craving within grew greater and greater. Each pair of long legs, each pair of curvaceous breasts that I saw made me need and desire more. I wanted to touch, to feel. I wanted to have. I couldn't help but leer at them. I still felt an edge from the arse kicking I'd delivered earlier and now my hormones were working double – no, triple – time.

Night would soon fall, so there was an increasing urgency to find shelter. The sky had that grey-blue tint to it that appears before darkness fully takes control. A number of street lamps had sensed this and so glowed redundantly. This place, after what had happened earlier, could only be home to me for a day or so, despite how perfect it seemed with shelter and so many hot women nearby. In a place so small it'd be impossible to avoid everyone in that group – I didn't even remember what they all looked like; only the skinhead stayed fresh in mind, but something told me that not one of them would forget me.

I couldn't face another night in the open, so I took another risk. I made my way back to the park. The hut, despite being only a flash in my memory, had looked perfect for a night's rest.

If I could get into it I knew I'd be laughing. I just hoped the area surrounding it would be free from people, especially that gang.

Relief shook my hand when I got there and saw no sign of them. The journey back had been quiet – only a few workers making their ways home. I looked up at the hut's roof and noticed some kind of mildew. Then I walked around it and found a window that was ineffectually boarded up. I leant against it and peered through a crack in the wood to see inside. Some old tables and chairs from what I could make out.

I moved to the door – padlocked, but very rusty – and gave a push with my shoulder. I felt something give, so I took a few steps back and lunged through it. The lock gave way and I found myself inside. Again, my adrenaline was pumping. I was pleased with the success I'd had in finding the place, in getting inside.

Aside from the cobweb-ridden tables and chairs, there was a number of football goal posts pushed up against a wall, of which one had fallen towards the floor and landed awkwardly on a pile of tables. There were two large buckets loaded with goal post nets and flat footballs. Pots of paint were piled into a corner, their colours indiscernible due to the dust and faded light. A collection of clipboards sat on another table.

The sound of a female cough coming my way stirred me back to life. I sprang to attention like a well-trained guard dog. It was my new territory now.

My body took control and quickly stepped to the boarded window and peered through the cracks to see who was coming.

The hairdresser. I recognised her instantly. She was coming towards the hut. So she was coming towards *me*.

As if by instinct, I veered outside and pushed the door in behind me. I had no idea why or what I was doing. *Puppet on a string.* I leant on the door and smiled, revealing my crooked teeth. Suddenly, I left the shack behind and walked forwards, round the side of the hut into her direction. I moved into the open and saw her. *No one around; only the hairdresser and me.* I stood perfectly still. She was looking at the ground as she came forwards, but her eyes rose hastily when she sensed a presence.

She gasped for a second then gave a quick laugh beneath a concealed smile when she saw merely a boy in front of her. "Oh, you frightened me," she said, almost embarrassed.

Hmm, I was embarrassed earlier too, because of you.

She had curly, shoulder-length brown hair and I remembered the view I'd had of her in the shop. *Our view of introduction.* She was quite a bit shorter than me, but she had incredibly tanned skin and deep dark eyes. Quite seductive, really. Her smile was almost too pleasant for a moment. "I'm sorry. I feel so stupid."

"It's okay," I said.

She squinted as she took a closer look at me. "Wait a second. I know you. Well, I don't, but... You were looking at me. In the shop window, earlier."

Was she mocking me?

Maybe I blushed.

Maybe she saw that, so she added, "You know, that was kind of cute. Why were you doing that? Looking at me, I mean."

I almost wondered if she was flirting with me. I decided to play along with it, even though her age made it a ridiculous possibility.

"I liked what I saw." This made her giggle. "And I still do." This made her stop.

Maybe she remembered I was a stranger.

Stranger.

"Well, thank you," she adds after a pause. "Anyway, I really must be going."

She sidesteps then moves forwards in an attempt to pass me. I turn as she goes by me, start up and move in tandem with her. I don't need to say anything. I don't even need to look at her to know, but I can tell she's making uncomfortable, hopefully discreet, glances at me. She's desperately unsure.

Without hesitation, as we pass the door of the hut, I grab hold of her by the shoulders and throw her into the door. As she passes me, I put my foot out. She trips over it and falls headfirst into the door. She manages to cover her face with her hands, but the door swings open on impact and she lands inside. I move in

38

behind her, lift her by the hair and throw her further into the space. She lands on her back and I notice blood dripping from her lower lip. I slip on top of her stealthily, very stealthily as Poe would say, covering her mouth. She doesn't make a sound. Maybe my hand prevents her from doing so, I don't know. I'm on autopilot now. My chest presses hard against her breasts – taut and succulent – and I feel myself come alive.

Jodie. Her body.

It's out of my hands now.

Before

They always say they can help you. They don't know shit. Fight it, they say. You can fight it. We can fight it. You can fight it. And I tried to fight it, believe me. I tried to fight many times. But I was too weak; I was so weak I fell right back into what I'd left behind.

In the beginning it was the streets or rehab. The streets first. I thought I could brave it out. But it was the streets for too long. Another two years after I met them and began to work with them and the one who'd looked after me, cared for me and protected me had gone. Dead from an overdose. Fucking drugs. They fuck you up and kill you.

It shook me up. She'd been my mother figure. She'd taught me everything I knew. How to look after myself. How to be independent. It's tough on the streets.

But she was dead. And I was with her when it happened. She leant down, placed a rolled ten pound note up her nose, the same as always. Inhaled deeply. Exhaled deeper. Lots of sniffing. Her eyes rolled around. She reached for the bag of powder and threw it to me. I tucked in.

The needle came next. It sunk deep into her arm. As she pressed down, her eyes bulged. She still felt it, even after all these years. Her eyes watered as she released the needle. Her face and body began to tighten.

I did a line and fell onto my back. From the ground my eyes met hers. She started to shake. I watched. Her eyes lost their whiteness; I watched red filled the gaps. I smiled at her. Snot dripped down her nose. Sweat covered her face. She was, in an instant, like a child. All I felt was my eyes – heavy. She flopped into the chair. My eyes closed.

I still mumbled to her as I was barely conscious. Every time I woke up I cranked inaudibly into the night's air. She looked alive, stoned as I was.

She was dead.

Eight Years

At one year old, sleeping in a makeshift cot had to do. In from the hospital and put down, his mother sparked up, ignoring the cries of hunger. She opened the door and business resumed as normal.

At two, just the same, but walking.

At three, he started to learn that movement meant getting in the way, so he kept still. He sensed where he could be and when. Noises told him when it was time to hide and when it was safe to come out.

At four, he understood that bad things were happening. Mummy was on the bed. The angry man, the one who'd slapped him, was on top of her. But the little boy couldn't understand what this older man – grey, ugly – was doing. He could see part of the man's body had gone inside his mother's. He was making odd noises, whimpers. His mother clutched at a pillow and stared straight at the ceiling.

A look to the left and the older man saw him as he tried to hide behind his favourite dirty rag. *Get the fuck out of here, you little shit*, he shouted, and he threw the other pillow towards the door. The little boy scarped.

At five, the men kept coming. Some would hit him. Some would touch him, stroke him. He'd cry every time; he had no idea why. And he'd see his mother lying there, the same as always. Occasionally, she'd shudder. She never wore many clothes, but the flat was always cold. He shivered every day as he woke up, as he played among the syringes, beer cans and gin bottles, eyeing the line of white powder as it lay half used on the battered coffee table. And he shivered as he went to sleep, his mattress strewn across the floor next to the radiator that was never on, the covers a different colour than when he'd begun using them.

At six, his clothes no longer fitted. Some of the men liked that. He hated how their hands felt: the dryness. If he'd cry they'd hit him. If he'd cry again they'd choke him. His mother never saw a thing; she was always on the bed getting fucked, her eyes fixed with a blank stare, only sometimes they were closed now.

At seven, when they came near him, he found a spot and stared too. He thought his mother was teaching him an old trick. She'd often be on her stomach now, a man above her, giving it from behind, another sitting nearby, watching; the third with him. Her eyes would be closed – definitely closed. She might even be asleep. She might have been dead were it not for the occasional groaning.

After the men left, she'd go to her son, scream about the mess and collapse in a heap next to him. He'd stroke her hair. It was always so sticky.

He was hungry. Hungry every day. He drank water from the kitchen sink tap. The plastic cups were grimy. He'd scratch at them. Mould would appear under his finger nails. Drink in hand, he'd play. He'd fly the needles around, imagining them to be the fastest jumbo jets in the world. He'd never been on a plane. He'd taste a little of the liquid that he'd find. It was nasty. Too sharp, too bitter.

At eight, oh at eight, he got it. The men kept coming, they kept fucking his mother, they kept groaning. And they kept screaming, punching and hitting: sometimes the furniture; other times, his mother. Him. And he knew what he didn't want anymore: he didn't want the men to come near him. He'd bite them, their hands, anything he could reach. And they'd hit. Sometimes blood would drip down his cheek. On his chin. Over his clothes. One time he couldn't open his right eye for weeks. The pain killed him. But during that time, there was a saving grace – the men stayed away.

When the eye opened up, though, they were back.

That was when he was just eight: a child unable to share the tears that wanted to stream out.

Approaching his ninth year on this blessed earth, the door opened to three people he hadn't seen before: two men and a woman. They picked him up and took him away. They didn't say where they were going and he didn't ask. They didn't even tell him who they were. Without knowing it he was happy to leave. His mother was still unconscious on the bed as he was carried out past her by the largest of the men. He'd never forget his final sight of her. She didn't know he was leaving; would she ever? Did she even care?

Looking back on it, he'd be sick one day. The future brings with it promises of so much. But with a past like his what more could you possibly expect for the future?

It's all right, they told him. *You'll be safe now.*

He didn't talk to them. He didn't even look at them. He was afraid of strangers: they might hurt him; they might touch him.

We're going to take you somewhere so that you'll be safe.

They couldn't have been further from the truth, for in the years to come safety didn't come from being elsewhere; safety only came from not being with Sean.

Before

"You can beat it. We can beat it. You *can beat it."*

    They tell you that to make you confident. So you'll believe you've got what it takes to be normal again. That is, if you ever had it to begin with. I sure as hell didn't.

    I woke up the next morning with my body squeezed against her bedroom wall. My face was numb. The sight that lay before me – her dead body, her face frozen stiff – will never leave my mind. Her eyes stared right at me, somehow horror-struck. Her eyes. My eyes one day.

    After she'd died and my life had been sucked away, I moved on. We'd spoken of Coventry in the past. The night life; the popularity of legs spread. What else did I have to offer?

    The other two, they'd gone. One, a year before; the other, when she saw the body. Who was I to her anyway? Coventry was all I could think of. Make a go of it.

    I lasted three weeks there. Black eyes, bruises, too much competition. If the guys didn't hit you the other girls did. I wasn't welcome on their patch. And every street I could find was someone's patch. Nowhere to be. Nowhere to work. No way to live.

    Day twenty-two, a black eye on my face, and I fell into a doorway. With a bottle of Jack I'd lifted, I drowned my sorrows. They rarely left me alone. It forever stung. The second eye closed and I slept. Passing out meant not having to face my life, the guys, the girls.

Earlier

I left her in there. She'd rolled onto her right side, kind of like in the foetal position, with her cheek pressed against the ground. That view, it lives with me night and day. What I'd done – worse, I believe, than any of the sins I'd committed before or have, indeed, since – was beginning to seep fully into my mind. As I pulled my trousers up, I buckled forwards on the balls of my feet as though someone had punched me in the mid-section. I struggled to breathe.

I'll tell you now, I derived no pleasure from the act. It was a release. And it brought about a sickness in me as I sat outside unable to move. I didn't get it; didn't understand how my body was reacting. I couldn't understand my lack of control. Until it was too late. Things like that haunt you and never let go.

Inside the hut when I came, it hurt. My eyes bulged and I thought I was going to be sick. And ten minutes later, it was still gnawing away at me. It's been six years and I can't tell you how much I regret doing it; as much as I regret life itself is how much. My mind aches at the thought, today more than ever. As soon as I could, I gathered myself together and ran.

At the other side of the park, near the swings, I collapsed to the ground, finding comfort in the soft tarmac, and I leant on the perimeter fence. Like a bird in a cage. I positioned myself so that I could see the hut. I didn't know why. But deep down, something made me stay, watch and wait. I beg you, it wasn't voyeurism. Instead, it had something to do with finally comprehending the consequences of my actions. I had to see her on her own two feet.

From this moment, even though I didn't know it, I was an empty vessel no more.

With my mind racing I managed to focus on the hut. But very soon my head went blank. To the outside world I probably looked like I was stoned. The truth be known, I was stoned – stoned by what I'd done.

I didn't feel regret. That came later, and in masses. Or if I did I simply couldn't identify it yet. Regret, it's a crazy internal choking that dwells on you. And it's necessary to survive.

My body didn't flitch. My eyes didn't stray from the hut. Time went by; indeed, the cliché *minutes felt like hours* rings a bell. A few people wandered by in a number of directions, unaware of the carnage they were passing, and darkness came down as if the heavens collapsed.

I waited. For what, I knew not. Her, I guess.

She didn't come.

After more time dissolved into nothingness, birds made the final chirps of the evening as they retreated home. I heard cars in the distance. I heard my own breathing, slow, shallow. Hearing these sounds brought me back to life. I got up, unaware of where my legs were taking me. Unaware of why, too.

I soon figured out where. Why, though, was a mystery.

As I stalked nearer the stained haven, I tried to make out sounds from within it. Only silence prevailed. I checked the park and field out with a quick glance. Again, nothing. That was a positive; I needed to be alone for this. *Alone, that is, except for the hairdresser.*

I reached the hut's door. A crackling noise behind me. I spun around, half expecting some of the guys from earlier to be there. Nothing. Then more noises. My eyes scanned, my body braced itself. It still hurt but I was ready.

Another rumbling in the bushes, then I saw it. A squirrel. I had to regain my focus. The door was in front of me. It wasn't completely closed, but the gap didn't provide me with space to look past.

I had to take the risk. I cautiously lifted my arm and pressed my hand against the door. Stealthily again, but for a different purpose. The door moved inwards a fraction. That was all I needed to enable me to see inside. A glance over both shoulders and I saw all was clear. I moved so close to the door that if it were freshly painted the fumes would have been overpowering. I peered around the door like a caring parent quietly checking on a scared child after bedtime when the bogeyman is on the prowl. Would I find a child tortured by a nightmare? It was likely.

Seeing it all helped me understand finally. The room was well lit by the moonlight now and I entered from the shadows. I saw her, still lying in the same position, exactly as I'd left her, as though life itself had frozen the moment I'd exited. She didn't move and I couldn't see nor hear breath escape from within her. I wondered if I'd killed her and the sense of dread and panic returned. *Should I check her or should I run?* I asked myself repeatedly. The word *murder* imprinted itself on the inside of my eyes, and every time I blinked and closed my eyes there it was staring at me. *Killer. Life taker. Predator.* I could have been labelled anything, more dangerous and hated more now than ever. The lifeless body before me led me closer to the fiery hell beneath my feet. My gaze drew along her body, unable to move, the sexual thoughts I'd normally have called upon gone, even though I willed myself to do so. I tried to look at her hair in the same way, hair that was once flowing so radiantly in the wind, now carelessly strewn across the cold ground. At her strength-sapped shoulders, once so strong, now rounded and old. At her rear, once such a turn-on, now as repulsive as I myself were. And at her defeated legs, once bounding along the catwalk of life for all to see and admire, now without strength and incapable of movement. I tried to cover my mouth to prevent a car wreck of a sound from escaping, but I couldn't. My hands refused to move.

I had done this.

A loud gasp, a bucketful of air carrying a lifetime of screams inside of it, shot its way through my body and released itself. A hoarse nasal sound, half a child's empty whining cry and half the sound of a fog horn. And it made me feel and realise I was the lowest of the low.

Then something happened. I saw movement. I inched forwards and saw it again. Her body moved. It actually moved.

The noise I'd made had stirred it to life. Then more. Big movements as it shuffled on the ground as if my voice were a battery pack controlling it. I heard a muffled sob, not dissimilar to those I'd heard earlier, once so fresh to my ears, now degenerate and stale. Her body tightened into a harder ball.

I didn't think, *She's not dead!* I didn't think anything you'd expect. The sight flustered me. I couldn't take my eyes off her, in the same way a cinema audience is transfixed by an epic. Until now my eyes had been fixed on women as objects, means by which to fulfil needs and desires. Only now, I saw a helpless creature, pitiful and damaged. I recognised devastation like I'd never seen it before and it jumped down my throat. While looking at her, all I saw was what I'd done, what I'd caused. The act and the effect.

With her eyes to the ground she screamed. I stumbled, startled, and backed off. My heart pounded and I ran again. With no place to go. I couldn't look ahead and I dared not look back. But the scream, I heard it ring on and on. Even when I was far away, it still rung on and on.

*

I ended up sleeping behind a wall at the end of a street I'd come across when I was close to giving up and sleeping on the pavement. The wall backed onto some trees and was filled with mud but it was late, so I settled for it. The street before it was crammed full of identical houses. All semi-detached with three windows in total on the front: two downstairs and one large window upstairs. They were unsightly. They needed four equally positioned windows to look regular, but instead they stuck out like sore thumbs. Some of the gardens, however, fared better. Trees, bushes and flowers adorned them. In summertime they must really come to life. Altogether different from the death throes of now, when colour was faded and bareness dominated.

This wall, I discovered it by chance. After leaving the hut and its contents behind forever, I walked the streets when my ability to run abandoned me, much like a homeless person

49

without destination. It must have been the early hours of the morning when I came across this street, Hillway Close. My body reeked of exhaustion and I'm sure I stank. I craved rest too. With each step my body dug further into the ground. I had to stop. I entered the street ready to sleep anywhere. Hide behind something. But I only found filth. I was about to give in to the muck when I rounded a bend in the street and saw the wall standing before me. A dead end for most but a beginning for me, it ran from one side of the street to the other. I couldn't see over it, but there was space to pass through between the wall and a bush on its left side. Trees towered above and went far into the distance. I dropped onto the ground, a heavy load. My eyes rammed shut. Sleep came to me in seconds.

*

The side of my face was twisted against the wall's rough surface. The shape of the upper part of my body was equally as awkward. Nonetheless, I managed to sleep and it was hours after I'd parked myself, numb from my mind's wanderings and the cold. It was a bitter night – dry, but with a biting wind – much unlike the previous night.

The hours I slept were filled with an endless stream of dreams. I met myself in them, the moment in sleep when one is utterly powerless. There I was in the same place, my face twisted against the wall and my body equally uncomfortable. My hands dug deeply into the grass and soil. For comfort or as a result of fear, I had no idea.

I was looking down on my mangled form from up above, not as far as the heavens, wherever one might find them, but from above the trees, deep into the night's sky. I was giving the boy down there a disapproving shake of the head. And I was slowly regaining my power, sure I would one day touch the gods, when the boy's eyes flicked wide open. In barely a second they shot open like somebody from afar had pressed a remote control. Reality television, and he had me. I watched him stand up and brush down the grime that had collected on his clothes. He didn't

50

shake off the discomfort he must've felt and he didn't slow down. He just got up, took three steps to his left, and emerged from behind the wall. I followed, floating above his head, distant as a helicopter, yet I could make everything out clearly and I didn't bother to be cautious. He wouldn't see me following, I was sure of it.

As I followed my replica's steps with anticipation and apprehension, I felt weightless and began to feel powerless again. Where was he going?

He left the road and so did I. I expected to feel queasy as I flew with the seagulls, but motion sickness evaded me. The sense of weightlessness was actually exhilarating for a time. It was like I'd been walking in a desert for five days, parched and malnourished, when I'd finally come across a fountain of water and a pile of food. Before finding it, my mind had started to crumble; things weren't really there, despite what my imagination told me. But with the fountain before me and the possibility to drink limitless amounts of water staring me in the face – I may even have dived right into the fountain, allowing its beautiful juices to soak into my skin – I was able to see the complete picture: reality and its consequences. I even felt alive, an omnipotent eye from way up here, yet still somehow ignorant of the truth.

The boy below walked while I glided. The route he took was familiar, one I'd taken before. Recently – too recently. Realising, the feelings that consumed me because of my new-found mystical powers ran away like a bandit fleeing the scene of a crime, like bath water desperate to escape down a drain. Instead, panic and a formidable desire for freedom lunged at me. I couldn't parry, I couldn't defend, I couldn't even control where I was going, for I was totally powerless to stop all that came at me, all that attacked. I tried unsuccessfully to veer off course, desperate to follow him no longer. But the more effort I put in to change my flight plan, the more my body was restricted. I was stuck on this trail – perhaps even this course – for life and there wasn't a thing I could do about it. My muscles contracted, my face became tense and I tried one last time to push away from the place to which he was taking me. I knew where he was leading me. It had to be. Like a dog on a leash I was being controlled. And I'd lost the fight.

In a sweeping motion I was drawn closer to him. He walked briskly, his hands in his pockets, a midnight walker, one without a dog, out and about to clear his mind, his thoughts, for some think-time, and he whistled a happy tune. Yes, he was whistling, the sick bastard.

Automatically and involuntarily, my body nose-dived all the way to the ground, coming to a stop a metre from it, again through no choice of my own. I wished I'd hit the ground; I wished I'd killed myself; that way, it would've ended and I would've been shown no more. But, no, it continued, and full on. I was almost made to walk behind him, save for the few feet that separated me from the ground. Still, his pull on me was immense and my body was drawn to him, like a young child to the biscuit tin.

To that fateful place, we went – he chirpy; I ready to make space for myself in hell. I wanted to scream, *He's coming, watch out*, but my mouth wouldn't open. I put my hands to my face to check why my voice was restricted. Wires covered my jaw, shutting it tightly, and I wore a Hannibal Lector mask – all the trimmings. For real psychos only. *But I'm trying to help. Stop!*

Too late.

He went inside the white hut. I hovered several metres away outside, my arms outstretched. I heard noises as he moved around inside, then I was turned fearfully to my right. That was when panic rose to sheer terror. I was an elevator falling fast, expecting to hit the basement floor, waiting to be crushed. But it didn't hit. No matter how far I fell, it didn't happen. I just kept falling.

A cough and she was by my side. We were both stranded. We were falling towards hell in unison.

With my hands outstretched I was pulled away and up, just higher than a person could stand. Then the final cough. The hairdresser was approaching. *God, no. It can't happen.*

He came out again, walked to her and the surprise made her jump. She giggled and they exchanged some chatter. They even looked like they were flirting with one other. I couldn't hear their words even though I was only metres away, but I could make out their faces clearly.

Now she looked worried and my heartbeat increased tenfold. She started to move off. He walked by her side. I told her to run, I shouted it to her, but she paid no attention to my silent words. The mask stopped everything from coming out. As they passed just below my feet, I tried to reach out – to grab him and stop him; to grab her and save her.

Save her.

But I can't reach. My arms are glued to my sides. I try a warning scream. Only a muffled sound comes out.

They're next to the door. It's about to happen. I'm ten steps ahead of them. My eyes are spread wide. He wrestles her by the shoulders and pushes. They're inside. I wince at the way she falls to the ground. The door blows shut behind them, leaving me alone, out in the cold.

I shake, writhe, desperate to free myself. Unsuccessful.

The air around me goes silent: no cars in the distance; no wildlife; no life. The only sound comes from within the hut. I hear a tussle and, still, I struggle to move. Struggle to do something, anything to stop this from happening. I hear another loud noise and she screams. Her scream pierces my soul. I want to clutch hold of my heart, but my arms won't move. I can't reach the pain I feel.

I sustain the pressure and try to force my jaw open. The force eventually makes my mouth fly wide open. The mask tears away from my face. Pieces of wire drop but evaporate before they reach the ground. I scream, finally, the kind of scream that would wake a dead city. She has to hear me. Someone nearby has to hear me to help her. Surely they'll come.

But they don't. No one comes. I know they won't for I've lived through this before. I already know the ending. Nonetheless, I wait, screaming for help, unable to gather the help she desperately needs or even move myself. I'm alone, just like them, and unable to get there.

I fight my body and manage to stretch my arms out. They fly away from my sides as if wood has been snapped. I reach out to the hut, but my body still won't move to it, no matter how much I urge my limbs to move, fucking move.

The wind suddenly blows fiercely and I'm rocked. I can't keep steady. My body swings and I feel violently sick. Bile builds up in my mouth as I hear another scream, a scream of pure terror, of human agony and suffering, of corruption, of invasion, of violation, of destruction. Imagine a city bombarded by war. Imagine this.

Another severe gush of wind and the hut's door blows open. I can see their legs, their feet, his on top – I recognise the shoes he's wearing as my own. His legs are moving; hers are still. Like she's given up, the life force removed from within. The sick fills my mouth now; it's dripping out. Like a baby at the dinner table, I can't wipe it away.

Then the foundations shake. The building, it's fucking shaking. The roof blows off. Then each wall in turn, a piece at a time, comes away. I heave and the puke covers me. Even though I feel empty, it's like there's an explosion in there. It's choking me and I shake more, violent thrashings from side to side. I think I'm in the throes of an epileptic fit. But among it all, I can still make them out. Despite everything around me and despite being thrown around by the gale, he won't stop. He's unaffected by the wind as it howls in rage above them, twisters forming at all corners of the field. He moves as wildly as the wind itself. His arse is pounding and she's stopped moving.

I scream again, a single breath, like a well-trained singer, that lasts a lifetime and will never go away. As the hallucinating sound consumes the neighbourhood, he still continues, oblivious. My body starts to pull away, even though I want to go closer to them. I'm raised higher and higher, but I don't stop screaming. Their shapes grow smaller, but I can see them plainly. My arms reach out to them as I travel in the opposite direction. My scream continues to reverberate in the night's air, but I can only see them clearly. They become even smaller, minute, the size of pins, the size of ants, but they remain in view for me to see. They won't leave me, nor I them, and he won't cum, the stubborn bastard.

Bright light fills my lenses and I can no longer keep them in view. Bright light fills the space around me. I have to close my eyes, it's so bright. I can't see anymore, yet my scream lingers on.

The sun is behind me, my eyes are closed and I can still see them. I'm desperate for the image to disappear, but I see them clearly in my mind. I see myself down there. Fucking. The only one fucking. It's imprinted on the insides of my lids. I'll see it forever.

The heat intensifies as I'm turned around and led towards the sun. Thousands of miles up. On and on and up. As I near the sun, my skin begins to peel away from my body. Liquid forms and drips down my face. I'm disappearing into thin air, but the vision of what I've just witnessed and done remains with me. The vision of my mind, as I melt and vanish. I leave, but it stays.

*

I awoke with a start, face downwards, choking on the dirt. I was out of breath, like an unfit runner. Discomfort beyond comprehension reigned over my body. I was overrun by heat. Sweat, which I initially mistook for rain, covered me. My whole body. My hair freshly showered but totally lacking freshness.

I didn't realise I was still screaming. I used my hand to force my mouth shut when the screams wouldn't stop.

I sat up against the wall. My eyes welled up. Tears mixed with the sweat and streamed down my cheeks. Salt water seeped into my mouth. I looked at my hands – black, nails filthy – and imagined them strapped to my sides. I felt around my mouth for a mask. Any sign of it. Then I raised my head to the sky above. And I saw a familiar place.

You did that.

I screamed again.

After Eight Years

Still at eight: with the nuns of St Anthony's. A waiting game, waiting for the unknown, for what he was told would make him whole: a family. Made to read. Read and read. He rebelled and refused to read. Told to read the Bible. Read about his saviour. Beaten if he didn't. Beaten by the Fathers and the nuns. Just like the other men used to beat him.

Eventually, he read. When he realised there was nothing else to fill the days, except thinking or praying, he read. Read and read. He read the Bible – three times through – read Louis Stevenson and Defoe, read all those the nuns could throw at him. At first, he understood little. The nuns didn't have time for much but had plenty of time to pray and talk about the books they made him read. And over time he understood more. He encountered characters and stories that could only have come from the deepest of imaginations. Then, privately, he discovered different worlds altogether. With his small weekly allowance, he saved and started out on Allan Poe, made his way to King and tried to grasp Wilkie Collins. Stories of lust and murder and obsessions and revenge – stories with bite that brought out the goose bumps, which made the fancy pirate ship tales and stories of real life look stone-cold boring, uninspired and ridiculous. These dark worlds, he escaped to them every day. They taught him something new about people, about how we relate to one another. The hurt he encountered in them, he recognised from his own life. The hurt he'd never forget, never escape. *So others feel it too*, he was relieved to find out. He had to read more to make sure he really wasn't alone. He discovered all kinds of people when he read Poe's characters, and Greene's characters, and Conrad's characters: the old man whose eye vexed and the beating heart; the teenage gangster Pinkie Brown; and Kurtz, the man who dominated by fear – people, for to him they were as real as real got, to whom he could relate; people he understood. Reading about Patrick Bateman gave him a hard-on and he had no idea why. These characters had power like all those men in his past had power over him and his mother, power which his mother didn't and never would have – and he craved it to be his.

By nine, he understood what you could achieve with power. He was impressed by it. The majority of his days were filled by reading. Book after book and no more of the fancy shit the nuns brought to him. They tried Shakespeare on him. Yes, *Macbeth*, yes *King Lear*. But he sneered at the likes of *Much Ado*, of *Midsummer*. The gripping plots, the murderous villains, the deception. That was what he wanted. He might not have known all those things in life yet, but he could handle them in his mind. He liked them.

The day his reading was interrupted was the day he became different. The day the Fathers and the nuns said goodbye to him – the day he was ten – he was lost somehow. Not the guidance they thought they'd given him – no – but the freedom he had by being left alone to read material of his own choosing.

Why you looking at this shit? the first foster father asked him, ignorant of a lot of things. *Get rid of it. None of this crap's gonna be in my home.*

The head of the Masters family, uneducated, ignorant, selfish. A last ditch attempt at housing a boy they couldn't house. No one had wanted Sean. Two-and-a-half years, they'd tried. He was taking up a valuable bed, one which would be used to support local kids in trouble until they were put back on the right track. It's not that there weren't many prospective takers. They came in their droves. The trouble was as soon as his history was discussed with them, they high tailed it out of there. No one wanted to know him, no matter how little and desperate he seemed. No light for his future. Until the Masters visited one day. On paper not the best of families to be going with, but if they were the only one offering, what choice did the Holy Mothers and Fathers have?

And it kicked off immediately. On day one, the arrival: the announcement of no more books. *Pansy's game. Try sports instead.* On day two, shouted at for asking for too much food. For, you know, one *can* have too much. Day three, nothing happened, for he kept to himself: he went to the dinner table when summoned; he washed his hands after pissing; he went to bed when *Bed* was called; he didn't say a word. On day four, he asked to go to the park. It was almost his eleventh birthday; perhaps they'd be nice to him. He got a right hand for that. He tumbled to the ground, almost knocking the scotch bottle off the coffee table. On day seven with his saving grace – the family – as he reached for a plate from the cupboard, for he now prepared his own lunch, he lost grip of it. It smashed into three pieces. White, *Ikea*, cheap. Ron Masters came at him for that. As soon as the plate rumbled against the floor tiles, he heard Masters coming, so he ran for it. He ran into the living room, past Marie Masters and right into the clutches of the master of the house. He wriggled, but it was no good – the big man was too strong. A right hand connected with his hip. *You will pick it up, my boy. Up, up!* And he was dragged back into the kitchen. As he was thrown towards the broken pieces, a hand smashed against his back side. The blow sent him onto his stomach, right onto one of the two remaining pieces of plate. His elbow cut open and the piece he'd picked up fell. Three further pieces appeared before him as it collided with the floor and broke up. *Stupid boy. Look what you've done now.* For good measure, for clarity, for whatever reason, the right hand met him again, this time on the small of his back. He cried from the pain, his lower jaw rolling back in on itself. The big man stumbled off into the distance, leaving nothing behind him but rubble. Day nine was his eleventh birthday. The wounds from two days before hadn't even begun to heal. He hadn't picked a book up in four days – the last time he was caught with a book, on day five, he'd been hit – and he felt vacant. They'd bought him a birthday cake and he'd been promised it after lunch. Lunchtime came and so did the little boy eagerly. *You've got no patience, kid,* the foster father grizzled. But he got to cut the cake. He ate a piece, smiling. He ate a second – wolfed it down, actually. *Greedy git*, he was called. He didn't care. He went for a third, all fingers and thumbs, thrilled that he could eat what he wanted for the first time since arriving. A lump of the chocolate icing fell onto the table cloth. *Pick it up, boy.* He picked it up, but it smeared, leaving a stain behind. *Look what you've done.* Masters' eyes bulged at the stain and his wife protested. In response his right hand flew into her cheekbone. She landed on the nearby sofa. *Look what you've done,* the man bellowed again, taking the little boy by his ear. *Look. But you want more? You still want more?* He pushed the child's face into the newly cut piece of cake that sat on his plate. It squashed as his face pressed down on it. He breathed pieces into his nose and choked. Coughing, he tried to lift his head up, but the man's hands were still applying the push. *You still want it?* The child was calling, *Please*, but the sound was muffled in the sweet. *Eat it!* Violently, his head was yanked free, but too hard, and he ended up on the floor next to the sofa. He wanted to clutch Marie Masters' feet but he dared not. The big man stalked over him, the bogeyman hovering over the child cowering under the duvet, and he cried for the monster to leave him alone. *Not again.* But he kept coming. He pulled the kid up by his hand. He threw him on to the sofa. His wife coiled up in defence and pushed the ragged doll of a child away and into the clutches of the giant whose hand clasped round his jaw. So tight – enough, the little boy thought, to crush his jaw and make his teeth fall out like crumbs. *More cake, you say?* The boy's head started to spin. His eleven-year-old brain was disintegrating. *The men were standing over him in his bed, on the sofa, in the bathroom. He remembered what they'd do to him, but he saw no faces. He saw only one face as he envisaged a hand coming towards him.* He opened his mouth the little way he could, allowed a finger to slip inside, *feeling the men's touch*, and bit. Bit hard. Harder than ever. Bit so much he felt bone, tasted something altogether and intoxicatingly new, and heard an unfamiliar sound: screaming, hurt. *They were touching him, their hands all over.* He clenched tighter and the mammoth came down to his level. *Never let go.* A blow to the head made him vibrate. *Their hands rubbing him.* Still, he gnawed. Another hit. *The men weren't there anymore.* This time he only saw bright colours. The finger in his mouth, his eyes closed. He didn't feel himself hit the ground as he went down.

Eleven-year-old Sean awoke in hospital, a nurse reading the chart that was hooked on the end of his bed, and he found the Masters to be gone, out of his life and merely a sticky memory of the past.

Tomorrow

I met Jimmy under a bridge. He was the kind of character you try to avoid in the street, but I liked him. He helped me at the time I most needed it, so I formed a loyal bond to him.

Jimmy was tall. He stood six feet high by the time he was fourteen. Now, at the age of nineteen, he towered over me at six five and I wasn't exactly in need of a few inches. He had short dark hair, which at the sides of his head had been almost completely shaved off. People said he was good-looking – he certainly had the ladies on his arm a lot – but I couldn't see it. His eyes had a suspicious tint to them like he was always asking questions of you in his mind and he barely cracked a smile, even though he was witty. He was forever working, I guess. His teeth were straight and gleamed of a shiny white when you could see them. Maybe that's what got the ladies going, I don't know. Night was his favourite time. It enabled him to blend into the background and vanish without a trace. He only wore black leather jackets.

Jimmy dealt drugs for a living. And a lot more, I found out later. He was very open about the drugs, at least with anyone who wasn't a cop.

"What score you after?" he asked me the first time we met, the first words he ever said to me. I couldn't afford anything, barely a coffee, much less something to stick up my nose.

I said we met under a bridge. That's particularly important. Bridges, much like trees in forests, slides in parks and walls in gardens, are ideal places to deal discreetly. Places to hide. When you look like I did – vagrant, defeated, guilty about the acceptance of life itself – you want to hide from the world and remain invisible.

As my scream subsided in Hillway Close, several neighbours came running out, in search of an attacker, of a helpless victim; whatever it was, I didn't hang around to find out. I got out of there like there was no tomorrow.

Every day after that, I moved. I tracked down anything that resembled shelter, in or under which I could sleep. Overgrown bushes, a bus stop, doorways had to suffice. To sleep with a margin of ease, I needed to disappear. My sleeping pattern changed, partly because I wanted to avoid being seen in daylight, but more because dreams haunted my sleep and I needed to avoid them. I couldn't bear watching the hairdresser approach the hut, so I caught a few hours in the day and roamed at night, a modern-day Nosferatu, only with no appetite now.

Without fail, each time I closed my eyes, I dreamt of the hairdresser and each time I screamed. I dreamt of Jodie too. Sometimes the hairdresser's face vanished and was replaced by hers. Two in one and life was unbearable. If I slept I'd wake up, soaked in sweat and stricken by guilt.

I travelled for several weeks, eating irregularly and taking my time. I hardly had somewhere waiting for me.

I'd lost count of the days, but on the day I encountered the river I smiled for the first time. A river bank brought with it all kinds of unexpected help. Shelter ranged from public toilets – usually too disgusting to remain in for more than the time it took to pee – to moored boats – fairly easy to break in to, or a sizeable deck on which to kip – to the aforementioned bridges, the greatest find of all. There were benches too, usually empty for the weather still wasn't up to much. And the river gave me a place to wash, not necessarily clean, but the hardened dirt scrubbed off to a degree.

Dozens of people passed me by as I walked along the bank, lost in my own thoughts, memories and dreams. Once in a while people passed me while I sat on the benches. And, for a moment, until they were out of sight, I was just like them. But seconds later, when they'd gone, I was me again and regretted it. I was missing out, of that I was sure.

Out of the blue one day, I came to the end of the river. I felt lost, unsure of where to go next. It couldn't be different. I needed the river. Time passed slower than usual and I lingered around without an objective. I was pointless.

Without much of an idea about anything in my mind I finally attempted to find the nearest town. I left the end of the river, which had become a friend, in search of life in a place where hopefully, somehow, a new life could begin. From where I stood by the river, I made out a path that led under the road – a bridge, perhaps one might call it an underpass, I don't know – so I headed to it.

I met Jimmy as I took my first step underneath it. He surprised me, but he wasn't surprised. He casually made his introduction. "What score you after?"

I knew what he meant. "I'm broke," I told him.

"Could be worse," he countered. "Could be dead."

"And that would be worse?"

From the look on my face, he saw I was serious and nodded. I saw on his face that he was serious too.

"Thanks anyway," I said, and I moved on into the semi-darkness of the tunnel. Two single, faded lights battled in vain to provide enough illumination to light the way.

He snorted a laugh. Or it may have been the cocaine talking. "Hold up," he called, and he jogged a few paces to catch up with me. "Stop a sec." I paused. He took me by the arm and I turned to face him. "Listen, you look like shit, I'll be honest with you. You need something?"

"I don't take drugs."

"That's not what I meant."

I wasn't listening to him. "It's not because of drugs I look like this."

"Hey, arsehole. Did you hear what I said? I know it's not. Now, you need something or should I move my drug-dealing arse along?"

He still looked deadly serious, but he almost sounded light-hearted.

I conceded. "I've got nowhere to go. I don't even know where the fuck I am. I've been sleeping rough for weeks now."

He smiled and his teeth lit up the tunnel, having a far greater effect than the failing lights. Was he laughing at me, or maybe he didn't believe me? To get him to believe me I said again, "I don't take drugs."

"But can you sell 'em?"

"What?" I asked, sure I'd misheard him.

"You dangerous?"

"What kind of question is that?"

"I've got a good feeling here. You need to get cleaned up." He held out his hand. "Jimmy, drug dealer. Pleased to meet you."

"Sean." He looked on, expecting more. I gave in again. "Fuck up. Good to meet you too." Our hands shook. His felt smooth – surprising. Our hands were oddly incompatible: his were gargantuan compared to mine; mine were battered by my battle with the wilderness.

"What are you doing here?" I asked. Stupid question, I now realise.

"You're not serious."

"You bail strays out often?"

He laughed. "Come on, Sean."

After that we left and started talking. Or he talked and I listened. I held onto the hope that he might help me more. Little did I know to what extent Jimmy would help and affect my life, both positively and less so. But at this point I was grateful because he was the first person to show any interest in me since I'd left the Andersons, discounting those who'd tried to kill me and those who would try to kill me if ever I crossed their paths again.

*

Jimmy didn't take drugs; he only sold them. He told me all about his *business empire*, as he called it. I was naturally sceptical. What I didn't know – believe, even – and what I'd soon find out was that Jimmy wasn't the average drug dealer you bump into on a street corner, someone with one eye fixed over his shoulder in fear of police action. Quite the opposite: in fact, he had a client list that exceeded three hundred names and an employee list of length. He didn't elaborate, but I got the impression that his paydays also came from other ventures too.

He led me to his home. To my surprise Jimmy still lived with his family: his parents and younger brother. His sister, he informed me, lived with relatives in America. The words escaped his lips with a longing of some kind.

En route, he guided me through several streets in which houses were the sizes of football pitches. Grand gates guarded residents. Cars in many of the driveways cost more than your average yearly salary.

"Where are we?" I asked him.

"Canterbury," he answered. He laughed to himself once more. "You really haven't got a clue, have you?"

I didn't answer, but it was pretty obvious.

He added, "Like a drifter in cowboy movies. So what you running from?"

He could read me like a book and he'd caught me off guard. I hadn't thought about what to tell and what to leave out, so I stalled. "What makes you think I'm running from something?"

"For a start you look like shit."

"That obvious, then?"

"So you gonna tell me or what?"

"I don't know. Life, I suppose. I fucked up and it finally caught up with me."

"When you going back?"

Unexpected, so I settled for the truth. "I'm not. That's not possible." It was his turn to look surprised. "I've got nothing now. Home can't be home anymore. I can't go back."

He waited for me to continue. When he saw that I wasn't going to, he encouraged me. "Go on," he said, softly.

"I've only realised recently, but the thing is, all my life I've destroyed other people's lives. Finally, through selfishness, desire, whatever – you see, I'm not even sure because of what – I destroyed my own life. I did something not for the first time, only this time it means I can't go back. And I just don't know what to do."

"Yes, you do," he countered. "Jimmy's here."

I used to admire people who used the third person when discussing themselves. Quirky or reassuring, I couldn't tell. Kind of like *Uncle Jimmy says everything'll be all right*, or *Granny loves you, you know that*.

Without a thought, I gave him a warning. "If you know what's good for you, you'll change your mind. You'll drop me like a dead fish."

"I do, and I won't."

"You'll regret it." I regretted saying it immediately.

"We'll see," he said. "We'll see."

He recommenced walking, signalled to me that we were on our way again, and I followed him, thankful he hadn't changed his mind, thankful he hadn't heeded my warning, thankful he hadn't gone off without me. This was Jimmy after all; I should have known better.

"This thing you done, you gonna tell me about it?" he asked.

Searching for an answer, I could only come up with one: "One day. I'll tell you one day."

"Be sure you do." He gave a thoughtful look. "But it's bad, right?" Now a cheeky smile.

"Yes, bad."

"Real bad?" he pressed. "Like scale it from one to ten. How bad?"

"Bad," I admitted. "Way up there."

"How way up there?"

"You got an eleven?"

"So, fucking bad then," and he clapped his hands together. "Can't wait. Don't be shy now." He changed course abruptly. "You, I think you could be as good for me as I could be good for you."

"What do you mean?"

66

"Business. It's all good in business. In time, Sean. In time."

And that was how I started working for Jimmy. A new life began. One of his hustlers, I was.

*

We arrived at Jimmy's home, a lavish house sprawled across a grand plot, complete with its own remote-operated gate and oval driveway.

Amazed by the beauty of his home and imagining the lifestyle that I supposed accompanied it, I asked, "Why deal drugs? You already have so much."

"And?" his sole response.

"Why risk it? If I had this… It's obvious you can have anything you want. Look at this place. You don't need the money."

"You mean," he corrected me, "*my parents* don't need the money. One word, my friend: independence. Another word: power. Fuck 'em." With that I understood him better than I understood myself. He hated the ways of the rich: the false posturing, the pomposity. He despised taking his parents' money. Besides, dealing was the ultimate kick in the teeth to them, the middle finger by which to rebel against his parents' ways. Fight off the hand that feeds you, so to speak.

To the self-titled Mummy and Daddy, Jimmy introduced me as a friend as I stood exposed in one of the house's many spaces, a six-piece suite assembled before me. *A friend*, Jimmy said, *who's gonna kip*. So I nodded, pleased to meet them, grateful for any help they gave or allowed me, regardless of whether it was forced upon them or not. I wasn't prejudiced against big money as, indeed, they may have been prejudiced against me. The smell that reeked from me – my look – would've put even a tramp off. Odd, though, that no one questioned why I needed to stay there. The truth was – and Jimmy saw this clearly – his parents didn't have, or wouldn't make, time for the family.

This meant that Jimmy practically raised his younger brother Steven who was eleven years old when I met him and – an understatement – impressionable. He idolised Jimmy. But no matter what he saw Jimmy do, I was in no place to comment. Just look at where I'd come from and what I was.

Their father, Richard Barton – *Call me Dick* – was the managing director of a national construction company called *National Constructions*. Business trips and late nights at work were the results. His wife Rosemary was born into money. Real silver spoon. Gold, maybe. She'd never worked a day in her life. When her diary wasn't filled to the brim with lunch appointments during which she discussed the latest fashions, or in-hair colours, or, of all things, the weather, from tennis lessons with her hunky instructor, to shopping excursions – normally in New York – she managed to find time to say hello to her children, but even then sometimes it was only done through a note on the fridge. Jimmy made his disaffection towards his parents clear to me from the outset. He always laughed at the fact that his parents' worlds would have come crashing down if they ever found out that many of the neighbourhood's most elite respectables were actually Jimmy's clients. This gave him great satisfaction. He vowed one day he'd tell them. What he loved was to see first-hand how the rich, the lowest breed in his opinion, could be even worse than the rest of us.

Jimmy's younger sister Sarah had escaped three years ago and lived with an aunt and uncle in the States. She no longer came home as often as she once did. I had no idea I'd ever meet her, much less the impact she'd have on my life. But that's a story for later.

I had to work hard for Jimmy, but I was grateful for every opportunity he brought my way. Drugs weren't his only game; there were several other areas of interest for him too, and he expected me to be involved in all of them, although he kept most of his plans for me to himself, filling me in as time went by, unexpectedly in most cases.

Any way of making a profit, he saw as a possibility and as such a worthy risk. Robbing an old lady's handbag was no problem; robbing a young lady's was fine too, just less frequent, the reason being, I think, Jimmy liked the ladies too much to miss out on a chance to get off with them. Stealing cars and selling them for parts was another; selling them to be cut in two, ready to be assembled into a new car, made to order. He had all sorts of contacts, too many I thought, and dangerous people; they were real gangsters. Taking the takings of a small newsagent or corner shop was still possible. Other shops were out of reach as a result of the technological advances in security. Banks in particular were a big no-go.

He told me how he'd got started: *Stealing sweets from a corner shop*, he said with a rare smile on his face. Lunch money at school came next. Knocking kids off their bikes and emptying their pockets. No one stopped him: kids, teachers, parents – none of them. Male or female, he wasn't prejudiced back then. One day he went the full whack. Stealing his father's pen knife, he'd made his mind up. He went to a corner shop in the neighbouring village, met the latest Indian family to grace the establishment, held the pen knife to the woman's face and delivered the well-rehearsed threats, not empty threats, but scare-the-shit-out-of-you threats. Intimidation was, and always would be, the key to his success. She emptied the till for him. He felt the rush that comes in such a situation for the first time and the motor of his life of crime was kick-started. He was only thirteen at the time.

As the years passed and the money rolled in at a greater rate, Jimmy tried to develop his means of income. So he put his hand into almost everything. I heard indirectly of his most dangerous sideline. Have a problem with a person, part with some cash, Jimmy's people sort it out. I asked Jimmy about it. *Not kill or anything, but, you know, we'd hurt people – hurt them badly – for the right price.* He just didn't get it and I didn't even try to help him.

Every time he spoke of the business his face looked docile, like he was telling a bedtime story when, in fact, he was telling me his deepest secrets. I felt like his confidante, the priest to whom he confessed, only there was no sorrow in any of what he said, no request for absolution and no pardon, that's for sure.

I didn't see it coming – perhaps naïvely so – but my basic role as provider of drugs quickly evolved into something more. I assisted with the robberies, the petty thefts – and I was there in the background when we took down the corner shops. I participated – I perceived I had little to no choice; no one said *No* to Jimmy – but I got nothing from it: no rush of excitement; no added adrenaline; no sense of undeserved power. But also no fear came; nothing shook me up then. When Jimmy spoke, you acted. There was no point in biting the hand that fed me. None whatsoever.

I was introduced to a number of regulars and was told to find more on my own; it was that simple at first. I dealt under Jimmy's bridge, by the river, in darkened alleyways full of putrid vomit and human waste – both kinds – and all around the darkest corners of the city. Sometimes I had to look hard. The underbelly exists, I believe, in every city. I dealt in pubs, in toilets, in clubs where security didn't add up to much, outside shops, sometimes those we'd taken down just weeks before. There were no limits.

On one occasion, Jimmy requested I find a change of scenery in which to deal. He named a local school. But I hesitated.

"Your job isn't to think about it." The first time he'd directed his harsh tone at me, although I'd been witness to it and its effect on a number of days gone by. "It's to deal."

"I know."

"So deal."

I thanked the stars that no one was buying that day. But that wouldn't have impressed Jimmy, so I buried some of my stash by the river, paid for it myself and took Jimmy the day's takings.

"Only one client?" he said nonchalantly.

I breathed a sigh of relief after solemnly nodding confirmation and he walked away from me. I was never asked to return there again. Like I said, in business he had no conscience. But I did.

Gradually my list of regulars grew and I became busy, much to Jimmy's approval. The saying goes, when the boss is happy things are better for everyone concerned, and it was true. Jimmy was a friend, yes, and he took good care of me, but when it came to business with him all personal ties were severed. You gave him what he wanted, no second chance.

I was given twenty percent from each sale I made, a sum not equal to the risks I took, I now realise, but money was money and I longed for every penny I could get. Best of all, the money was mine to do with as I pleased.

On my sixteenth birthday, some weeks after I'd learned about Jimmy's best money earner – pain for hire – he and a group of his friends – read, employees – took me to a high-class establishment for men – read, strip club – and the particulars of my job description went about-turn drastically.

I looked older than my years – I was six one and my build was strong – but I thought there was no way was I getting in. Little did I know, until we strolled by the bouncers shaking their hands, that Jimmy supplied the owner with his weekly fix and had the run of the place. With this guy I could go anywhere. He made me feel like a VIP – in the Players' Box at Wimbledon; courtside at the NBA Championship Finals next to Spike, Woody and Jack. He made me feel special like never before.

Girls with legs longer than you'd believe were everywhere. Like my switch had been turned on I sprang to attention. The club lived up to its name – *Xclusive* – with clients the best dressed in town and the interior out of this world. That's not to say it looked like a rats' nest from the outside either; quite the opposite. Men in suits sat on leather chairs and sofas, attended to with the greatest of care – attention to detail here – by blondes, brunettes, red heads, blacks, whites, Asian women, all hot as a blazing and uncontrollable fire, every taste catered for. This was a hypermarket of new proportions.

I stood in the doorway, my eyes wandering, dumbstruck.

"Put your tongue back in your mouth and don't swallow," Jimmy laughed. He slapped me playfully on the arm. "Come on," and he led me through the crowd to the bar.

The place was stylish. Neon lights filtered across the room, hanging from the ceiling and on the walls, advertising the beers and spirits for sale. To the right of the entrance, there was a stage. Parading on it, three women bounced this way and that, pouting at the men who sat a few feet below them, dicks up. They all wore thongs, different colours, and were braless. The men wore frozen smiles. A shiny silver pole was erected in the middle of the stage. One of the girls took hold of it with both hands, wrapped a leg around it and draped herself from it like a gymnast at the end of a routine awaiting applause. Onlookers pulled out notes and reached out their arms, keen to pry space between leg and thong strap in order to stash the cash in place. Perhaps cop a feel too. The women responded to each tip, I guess you would call it, by giving alluring looks and, a few times, air kisses.

I noticed one of the women on the stage dancing really seductively for a balding man. He sat below her. His moustache desperately needed trimming. She was dancing her heart out. Her cropped blonde hair, her breasts, her firm body were giving their all for this guy, this sad forty-something with a ring of notes held visibly in his hand. As she worked for him, I wondered about her life. A person with a family, a mother possibly, doing whatever she could to survive and support herself. Her child. The mother, they tell me, does it all for the kid. Apparently. There was something in her eyes that was absent in the other girls, something deep and painful. A longing, something in descent. Somehow, I found myself feeling sorry for her, and I didn't even know this woman. I found that oddly strange, mildly pointless. She continued to sway back and forth for this guy. She caressed her breasts and pushed her rear towards his face, barely any air between them. *But her eyes.* I still saw it lingering in her eyes. And for all her efforts for this guy, what did she get? Nothing. He gave her an extra long stare, then turned his attention elsewhere. A smug grin settled on his mug. He leant back in his chair and his body language read, *Not this time, sweetheart.* The balding guy: pleased with himself; the girl:

beaten, degraded. Then defeat turned to anger and she rammed a stare at him that sent bullets flying.

The dancer hated that man. So did I.

The woman backed off and headed to the next punter, ready to start over.

My attention snapped back to where I was when I heard Jimmy call to the barman, "Double vodka and coke. And a bottle of Corona." He turned to me. "What you having?"

"Same."

As he ordered for me, I kept glancing back to the bald bastard. There he sat, fistful of cash fraudulently at the ready, ogling the next dancer in the queue, using them. He wasn't going to give them a thing.

Jimmy was talking to me all the time, but I couldn't focus. My eyes darted everywhere. There was too much to see. I glanced back at the stage. The disappointed dancer had gone, maybe back to her daughter, back to real life.

The bar sat square in the middle of the room. Every type of alcohol available was lined up on shelves, which sat around the centre of the bar. Four walls of endless booze. Behind the shelves were mirrors that rose at least three metres in the air, undoubtedly so you could keep your eyes fixed on the talent on show behind you.

With drinks at the ready I followed Jimmy to the side of the room. I unexpectedly had two drinks – an odd mix of vodka and beer – in my hands. When we set our drinks down on the table, I took a glance back to the stage. Bald guy had gone too. Another punter, character unknown, had taken his place.

The chairs on which we sat were extravagantly patterned, although I'd dreamed of parking myself on one of the leather numbers. Posters of Marilyn Monroe, several other celebrities and scantily clad models were displayed on the walls surrounding us. We were in good company. The other guys hadn't come with us.

Jimmy placed his elbows on the table and edged towards me. "While we're alone," he began, "there's something I want to talk about with you."

"Okay."

"See, tonight there's something we need to do."

"Okay," I said again. To avoid the risk of sounding boringly repetitive, I added, "Want to tell me what?"

"Some work. There's this guy. Something we gotta take care of tonight. Can't wait, you understand."

"Here?" I asked. *It's my birthday, and now...*

"Here," he nodded.

He looked up and away from me. His eyes met with a leggy brunette. With raised eyebrows he signalled for her to come over. As she stepped closer, her hips swayed just right. When she was at our feet, Jimmy said to her, "Show him a good time," and he indicated me by a twitch of the head. She smiled and he got up. He kissed her hard on the lips, picked his drink up and said, "Enjoy." Then he was gone.

From deep in my seat I peered up at the woman who stood only a few feet before me. Like an embarrassed schoolboy who can't stand up for fear of discovery that something chemical has happened, I stayed where I was. She exuded sexiness. Her body was perfectly curved. I wanted to take hold of her breasts, but I was surprisingly too nervous.

"First time?" she asked.

"Never been here before," I mumbled.

"Just sit back and relax, and let me take you on a ride. This, I promise, you'll enjoy."

She stood knee to knee with me, higher though, took me by the shoulders, and lifted one of her legs over and round me. She came down on me hard and straddled my legs. I sighed. It was the most seductive experience of my life.

For five minutes, it must've been, her body swayed, it rubbed, it caressed. She was on my lap, grating her hips. I'd read about this when I'd been much younger, but little did I know what to expect. I'd never read about how to control yourself and I'd never been any good at self-control. I had an erection, more of a block than ever before, and I kept thinking about her reaction if she noticed it. Of course she'd already noticed it.

I tried in vain to divert my attention, but she moved faster, harder. I winced. A release and it was over. She got off me and planted her lips on mine. Her tongue entered my mouth and I trembled.

As she moved away, giving me a knowing wink, I sank back and saw Jimmy standing at the other side of the room. He was watching me and had a half-smile on his face. His teeth, again, sent the neon lights of the place crashing. He pointed towards the bathroom, helped my idleness by doing so, then signalled to himself. I understood what he wanted.

I went into the bathroom where I was met by marble tiling and golden trims. Aftershaves of every scent imaginable lay in front of the mirror and the attendant gave me a nod as I entered. I returned it, trying to act casual, uncomfortable as I was, then entered a cubicle and cleaned up.

Tommy Hilfiger awaited me after I washed my hands – soap applied by a stranger, towel placed in hand by a stranger – and I let the scent waft into my nostrils. *It's been a long time.*

I gave a tip and left to rejoin the others. When I reached them, Jimmy was whispering into the ear of an attractive redhead. He saw me and ushered her away with a finger.

"So," I asked, "what's wrong?" All the guys had smug grins on their faces. I told them collectively, "Fuck off."

I refocused on Jimmy.

"Come with me," he said.

With his back to me I recognised the bald head instantly. His hands were bound to the chair on which he'd been placed. His head was bowed down.

Jimmy had led me into a room that adjoined the bar area. I'd no idea what to expect, but I'd never contemplated being in such a situation. Noticing my stunned silence, Jimmy whispered, "You're one of us now, Sean. You're gonna know everything. You're gonna see everything. And you're gonna *do* everything. Welcome to my world. Something tells me you've got much more to offer than's been given so far. Prove me right, buddy."

"What are you going to do to him?" I asked.

"It's not what *I'm* gonna do, Sean. It's what *you* are gonna do."

"Excuse me?" I said, surprised even more.

"Fuck hasn't paid up, so he's gotta pay a different way." He spoke softly into my ear now. "Besides, he owes the owner of this place a lot more than he owes me, so we're gonna make sure he pays up. Kind of two birds, one stone thing. You know how it is." He raised his eyebrows at me. "Pass this test, Sean. Pass it and I swear there's so much more to come."

He walked away from me and went round to face the bald guy. He took one look at him and said, "You gonna pay, Gary Bevan? Wife: Mary. Three kids: Ricky, Margaret, Grace."

As soon as the name of the final child left his lips, Jimmy pulled back and sank a right hand into the guy's gut. The wind poured out of him. He couldn't cough or breathe. With a tilt of the head Jimmy signalled for me to join him. I obliged. Guiding me by the arm, he positioned me further round so that I faced the helpless man.

"This guy," Jimmy began, "can fuck you up twice as much as me. Now where's the money?"

The bald dick didn't answer. Inside I implored him to talk. *Say something. Don't make me do this.*

This.

Jimmy stands back, whistles a happy tune, and I know what I have to do. I hesitate to give the guy time to speak, but he says nothing. Jimmy shuffles on his feet behind me, anxious probably, testing definitely. There's no way I can let him down. But batter someone who means nothing to me? It means something to me.

I close my eyes and speak the only words I have inside my mind. "Why didn't you tip that girl out there?"

He laughs. "What?" His eyebrows rise. He laughs. He actually laughs. To mock me?

Barely a second passes by and my fist collides with his nose. Something gives: I feel cartilage collapse. "She worked hard for you." He kicks his free foot at me while he squirms in pain. "And you gave her nothing, you fuck," I shout, and I kick

76

him in the knee. I kick him again, this time in the chest, and he and his chair fall back. He lands hard on the floor. I stand over him and stomp on his chest, on his groin, and I get on my knees next to him. Using my hands, I lift his head two inches off the ground and punch him in the face. His head ricochets off the carpeted floor and I see stars in his eyes as blood covers my arm and sprays onto my face. I spit out the drops that go into my mouth.

I get up, walk to the door and get out of the room, without looking back. Not even a furtive glance. Trying to look casual on the outside, I'm a wreck on the inside. I've no idea what Jimmy's doing, but as I walk through the door I hear skin connect with skin, time and again.

As soon as the door closed behind me, I ran to the bathroom. My body shook violently, violent as I'd just been in there, my knuckles bled, and I promptly threw up into the toilet bowl.

What the hell am I doing?

After Eleven Years

So at eleven, Sean was back with the Fathers and the nuns. A different bed, a different room – one he had to share with another boy, named Davey – but he was back, taking up their space. They let him read, this time without checking up on him. There'd be no time for Sean. He was a number too many.

Davey was an unusual one. It took him three weeks to speak to Sean, the first and only time, never responding to a *Good morning*, never having the decency to show manners. He had ginger hair and his face was full of freckles. His nose was long – think *Chitty Chitty Bang Bang* – and his chin pointed. When he breathed, the room filled up with a quiet swishing, like the noise of the sea, except at night when the noise became a wailing, Sean could never tell whether from suffering or from pleasure. His screams woke Sean up every night. Like a car horn had been sounded by his bed, he'd dive up.

But in the third week, the time when Davey decided to talk to Sean for the first and final time, the loudest scream of all was heard. Sean's heart skipped a beat when his eyes opened to find Davey standing right over him. *Do you see it?* he asked, hysterically. *Do you?* Sean answered, *I don't understand.* Again Davey screamed, worse than a cat being mauled in a fight: *It's there, it's right fucking there.* *Ssh*, Sean told him. But the outrageous meowing continued. *Shut up. You'll wake everyone.* When all else failed, Sean grabbed Davey by the mouth, handled him like a rag doll, his hand also covering Davey's nose. Little Davey began to flounder, waving his arms dramatically. Sean just stared at him, eye to eye, as he suffocated the boy. It was only Father Jacob and the three nuns who'd stomped into the room to discover the origins of the screams they'd heard that prevented Sean from killing poor Davey. Poor little Davey. Poor, annoying, irritating Davey.

Needless to say, after that Sean and Davey were no longer on speaking terms. As roommates they were parted; something about safety being the number-one priority. Instead, Sean was transferred to some out-of-the-way broom cupboard of a room. It reeked of disinfectant, so recently had it been cleared out for him. No windows, just four close concrete walls, a bed and a table with a lamp upon it. It was here that Sean continued his reading; that his fascination with the perverse, the grotesque and the vulgar, much like the two lives he'd now left behind, grew. Each day, always by table light, he read. His command of the English language developed, his imagination flourished and his desire to read became insatiable.

It wasn't until he'd just turned twelve that Sean was finally rehoused. Another year and a half of wasting space but filling it the only way he knew how: with his mind and with his books. Chloë Miller and Simon Banks weren't married, much to the chagrin of the church, but they were financially viable and keen. The incident with Davey had been quietly brushed under the carpet and all looked to a positive connection between Sean and his new parents. Initially, it seemed that little could go wrong. The new parents quickly became devoted to twelve-year-old Sean, despite all the oddities they soon discovered about him: he hardly spoke to them; he'd snatch; he growled like a dog when he didn't get his own way or when he became angry; money frequently went missing from Chloë's purse; the cat disappeared.

Sean even started school – the regular kind that regular kids go to. Out went the daily religious education lessons taught by the caring nuns of St Anthony's; in came playground fights, lunchtime arse-touching, kiss chase, swearing, bullying and tormenting. Of course Sean played no part in games of kiss as he had no friends. He was an outsider from his first day stepping foot into the place. Alone but not lonely – for he had his imagination and his books, just as before – a loser, weird, all the names that kids call one another. Sean was sure he had these nicknames, perhaps more than others, but he didn't hear them.

Maybe that was because kids were scared of him. Perhaps it was because on his second day a kid one year older than Sean deliberately pushed into him in the corridor. While most to whom this happens cower in defence, Sean turned and, in front of dozens of fellow students, grabbed the kid from behind, placing his arm around the boy's neck, and punched him twice on the side of the head. As the boy lay there on the floor, quivering in agony, peeing himself, Sean undid the boy's belt and pulled his trousers down. Taking them from the scarred boy's legs, he walked away, happy as a prize pigeon. The other kid got all the humiliation. That got people talking. And that got people scared. And that meant the loner was left well and truly alone. Perhaps that's what kept him safe.

He was safe until the day he put himself in danger. Almost a year, he'd been there. They all still kept away from him. At this time, he sometimes craved friendship. Approaching the age of thirteen, he craved something else too.

He lusted after the tanned legs in the hallways, the skirts of the summertime. There was one girl: brunette, five four. She'd caught his eye shortly after his arrival. The same age, she was a popular one. Strutting around, she knew it; knew she caught the eye of many. Whenever she noticed a stare, she changed her plans and hung around longer. She liked being looked at. Sean saw this, so he wasn't shy about looking. With all but his tongue sticking out he'd follow her some days. From room to room at lunch, he'd see her chatting with friends, chatting up the cute guys, flirtatiously conversing with the younger teachers as they passed by. He even noticed some of them catch sight of her legs and like it. She'd notice him following her sometimes, and she'd smile. She'd move more slowly, suggestively, swaying her hips that little bit more, licking her lips, stretching as if tired. And he'd fantasise about fucking her.

As the weeks passed and became months, the skirts got shorter, as did Sean's patience. Seeing those legs – long, shiny, brown – he wanted to touch, to feel what the softness of a girl's skin was like. He wanted to put his hands in places they did in the movies he'd sneakily watched. And he wasn't prepared to wait any longer.

With nothing but the inkling of a plan in his head, he found himself following her as usual. It was time. Outside the sun shone brightly. Her legs came out as part of nature's course. And the tan had been worked on this week. Following her through the Maths block, along the main corridor that was decorated with graphs and bar charts and triangles proving Pythagoras' Theorem, he could smell her scent and it put him on heat. He walked faster when she said *See ya* to her two friends. She took this route all the time. It was always quite deserted around here. Plus the sun was out, enticing sports stars to strut their stuff and revellers to hang around in their cool groups. She knew he was behind her, he could tell: the hips, they moved more freely – too freely – and he gasped. Her magical powers grabbed him and he began to salivate. *Just one touch.* He reached out to her, his pace quickening all the while. She was none the wiser. Even though she felt his presence, she'd never give it away by looking back at him; that'd ruin her game and make it too easy. Without checking around, as she neared the toilet door, he came up beside her. As she took her final step to the door and put her hand out to open it, he shoulder-barged her and she slipped through easily enough. He followed her in with one big step and grabbed her. He touched, he ran his hand from the lower edge of the skirt upwards, and he sighed. He couldn't believe he was touching her. He was hard, in a daze. Grabbing her by the hair, he pulled her mouth to his and kissed her hard. Not defenceless, she bit, drawing blood on his lip, and slapped him. He didn't release the kiss. She tried to scream, only successful in making a muffled sound. He kissed and kissed, driven by a raging fire within; she resisted and resisted but couldn't break free.

As the door flung open, Mr Edwards, the Maths teacher who happened to be walking at the other end of the corridor on his way to lunch when he saw a boy push a girl into the toilets, entered and pulled them apart. Confused, for at first glance it looked like the boy and girl were making out, he ordered both to the head teacher's office.

Mr Edwards was only able to say what he saw. The girl, however much Sean denied it, claimed she'd been attacked, that she was in no way kissing her predator. Sean, fully in control again and no longer consumed by an over-sensitive dick, used his brain and came up with the perfect defence. Just like one from a story he'd read. The predator becomes the prey; the hunter, the hunted. She'd been flirting with him for months – others must have seen it; *besides, she's a tart and does it with almost anyone who'll pay attention.* A valid attempt to manipulate his superiors, one which made him feel smart. But a failed attempt. The shoulder tackle, Mr Edwards insisted, even through his confusion, looked violent enough to be proof. Unable to fully prove Sean's guilt, the head teacher decided to reassign Sean to a different school. The girl was left to endure months of counselling at the hands of a stranger in an attempt to resurrect the inflated ego that had just been so utterly deflated. To cap off being carted to another school, the perfect couple, Chloë Miller and Simon Banks, suddenly weren't perfect anymore. A claim of indecent assault – founded or unfounded, it didn't matter to them – was too much to handle and a call was made. They were out of there, so Sean was out of there.

Back to the thankful Fathers and nuns he went, but this time there was a surprise in store for all. Barely a week had passed by when a family visited: a father, a mother and their daughter. They wanted to help. You know, every town has its do-gooder. *Anything we can do*, they said. They looked around. They read some files. They met Sean. They read his file again. They talked about him to the resident psychiatrist. They were even told about the incident at the school. *Bet she stopped flashing that arse*, the father thought but didn't vocalise.

Little did the father know that in almost three years, when she and Sean would be fifteen, his daughter would go in much the same way as the girl at the school: short skirts, seductive poses, shapely arse. Little did he know that Jodie, as she sat not two feet from him, would also get into a tangle with Sean, that she would smile, and suck, and fuck. Little did he know what he was getting himself into when he, his wife and Jodie all agreed, *Yes, let's help him. Let's help Sean.*

Little did any of them know how it would all go desperately wrong. Before lust regained control. Before she fucked it up for him by fucking him.

Hours Later

There was nowhere to go, so I stayed in the cubicle for nearly an hour until the bathroom attendant asked if I was all right. Many people had come and gone, yet I remained.

"Surviving," I told him in response, and I feigned an element of discomfort in my voice to put him off the scent.

In reality I sat on the toilet, lid down, with my head in my hands. My knuckles stung. My temperature was burning hot. In the past maybe I could have hurt someone so badly without remorse but no longer. I'd changed and there was no way I was ready to go back to being my old self. But Jimmy and my work and the situation I was in were collectively pulling me back in the direction from which I'd come. And I couldn't struggle against it, for I relied on that life. I relied on Jimmy. Somehow, something had to change, but I had no idea how.

I decided to speak to Jimmy about it, little choice did I have. At least I knew he'd listen to me. The bond we'd built guaranteed that, I was confident. He might, however, completely dismiss everything I'd say, but it was worth a shot.

When I finally managed to compose myself, I rejoined the party, which was back in full swing. Several of Jimmy's guys were enjoying lap dances when I came out – funny how a man has only one face when a woman is straddling him: gleeful – and Jimmy was on one of the leather couches with the same redhead as before, only this time his hands and tongue were doing all the talking. No one was with them or near them.

I took the hint and chose not to disturb him. I knew better. Instead, I returned to the bar and ordered a couple more drinks. I settled down for the remainder of the night – it was still early by Jimmy's standards – at a table out of harm's way in the corner. The trouble was, I'd been at the centre of most of the harm tonight and thoughts of how easily I'd once again lost control raced around my head. I honestly thought I'd beaten it, but obviously I was wrong.

I became invisible, too young to be an attraction. I watched the night's entertainment from afar, but my mind was in a constant state of wander. I hadn't seen the bald guy come out from the room, although I'd been gone for a while earlier. I wondered what had happened to him and I found myself hoping, despite hating his guts, that he was all right. I wouldn't have the nerve to ask Jimmy later, so I kept checking the door out, willing him to somehow emerge and stroll out through it, although in all honesty I knew he'd need an ambulance to pull him free from that wreckage.

Despite the discomfort, time passed at a pace in line with time passing when you're out of it. I waited until the early hours and got up to leave. Most of the guys with whom I'd come, Jimmy included, had moved on to private booths with ladies of their choice – I thought about what stopped me from doing that and came up with too many answers to manage – so I didn't have to make any farewells and give any excuses for leaving at an inconceivably early hour or not getting wasted or even not getting fucked like the rest of them.

It was a night to remember. As I stood under the exit sign, bright and neon of course, I paused and checked the side door one final time, still eager to spot the bald guy, nameless no longer – even to see him teasing the dancers with his handful of bank notes again – but there was no sign of life. Gary Bevan – I couldn't see him, but thoughts of him wouldn't leave me be. The name would never escape me, even though he had.

*

I was flying again.

From high above the ground, I saw him as he got up and walked out from behind the wall, through the streets and into the park. From high above the ground, I watched helplessly as the hairdresser approached the hut, unaware of what lay in wait for

85

her, of what was only around the corner. From high above the ground, I couldn't stop him from destroying her, himself, me.

The next morning, I awoke in the spare room in Jimmy's house covered in sweat. My T-shirt and sleeping shorts clung to my body. I sat up and rested my head on my right hand. I felt so uncomfortable. Moments of the dream flashed in and out of my consciousness, more than ever before. I tried to shake it off, but my efforts were in vain. The only restraint from its vicious attack came when images of last night hit me even harder and broke me down yet further.

I brushed the duvet aside, exhaled deeply, got up, and left the room. I stepped onto the landing and opened the door to the next room along. As I walked, I passed photographs of Jimmy's parents at various functions, shaking hands with dignitaries of one kind or another, and generally looking very pleased with themselves. Smiling, I supposed, for the benefit of the camera and those looking on, eager to rub shoulders with anyone important.

The bathroom was the size of an average bedroom. I often wondered, why all the space in which to shower, shit and shave? Sea blue greeted me from floor to ceiling. A sea-blue carpet that felt warm between the toes. Blue bath, sink, toilet – complete with a fluffy cover, much like those you see on some nutcase's Mini's steering wheel – and bidet. The shelves, made of the same enamel as the bath, sink, toilet and bidet, were equally spaced apart and filled with hand soaps, body soaps, foot lotions, shaving gels, foam, oil, scissors, not blue, nail file, the same, eye brow plucker, nose hair trimmer; all the required tools of the rich were proudly on display. The shower curtain had patterns of waves on it and made me feel seasick and, on two walls, more photographs – keeping to the marine feel – were plastered. Various other six by fours were spread around on shelves and cabinet tops, highlighting the many beautiful sea views to which the family – or at least the parents – had been privy.

I stood in front of the mirror and leant against the double sink so that my arms locked. The sink unit was bigger than most office desks, fitted with gleaming taps that resembled old-fashioned ship door seals. I could see my shape in the reflection, but I couldn't make out the person standing there.

"What are you?" I said to myself. Whatever was there I couldn't come close to working it out.

Visions flooded in. I saw my fist colliding with his nose. I felt it give. I closed my eyes tightly and clenched my fists, edging the images away from inside, urging them to move on and bother someone else. They wouldn't.

I saw my leg kick him. I hit the sink with my fist.

I heard the slap of skin on skin as I left the room and I knew, just knew, what was happening to him. I clenched my stomach, preparing to vomit.

I couldn't keep reliving it like this. I slapped my face hard.

I turned the tap on – cold water; that was what I needed – and heaved a double handful at my face. I did it again, wishing away the frightful memory. And again.

When I looked back up at the mirror, I saw myself: water dripped down my face and onto my T-shirt. I took it off in one sweeping motion. It landed on the floor. My eyes were red; red from the cold water or as a result of tears that had welled up, I couldn't tell. I ran my eyes up and down my body. My chest looked quite good. Thin hairs poked through my skin, searching for daylight. My arms needed some work. My stomach, once flat, entertained deposits of fat now. Too much of the good life since I'd met Jimmy. I thought about how I could use my body. Built up some, it could be put to good use. Get to work – some kind of manual labour – and do something useful. *Something other than this.*

A final glance and I hopped into the shower in a pitiful attempt to wash my sins away and cleanse myself. The drain filled, the water ran down it, but the sins – every single one – stayed firmly in place.

With no desire for pleasure this morning I towelled myself off and stepped out. A few remaining drops of water dripped from my elbows onto the floor. The feeling of warmth as my feet reconnected with the carpet was instantly rekindled. I grabbed my toothbrush and went to work on the awful taste of the morning after the night before. I pushed hard to fight it off. Too hard and my mouth tasted of blood.

I lifted the T-shirt up from the floor and wiped a diagonal clearing on the mirror's surface, removing the mist that had gathered there and revealing my reflection. My eyes met its eyes. Disgust trampled over me. A bald head. A face, its nose crushed. I pulled at my hair. Anything to distract the recollection.

Searching around the sink, the razor jumped out at me. I picked it up and took a close look at it. *You could end it.*

The image in the mirror began to fade as mist hastily re-emerged. *The image*, I thought. *It could disappear forever.* I stared down at the razor as I held it in my trembling hand. *I could end it all, right here, right now.*

The bathroom door was locked. There were other bathrooms. Someone would find me but not for hours. No chance for help. No one to hear me scream.

No chance for redemption.

Could I ever make my life right? If the possibility were real – if, indeed, I could make up for even one tenth of the mistakes I'd made and the devastation I'd caused – I'd surrender myself to it, throw myself at it and thank it for coming my way.

And Steve. What if Steve were the one who found me? The number of lives I'd already tainted, I'd lost count. Not one so young. Imagine finding a body: the blood, the wrists slit, the motionless gaze from the lifeless eyes, the cold. I couldn't do that to him. He was a good kid. I couldn't ruin his life, not even in death.

Realising I had no choice, I dropped the razor, wrapped the towel around my waist, and left the bathroom.

*

Jimmy was lying on the bed when I returned to my room. I was surprised to see him. He didn't look at all the worse for wear.

"Hi," I mumbled, and I headed for the sole chest of drawers.

"So speak. How'd you make last night?"

Suddenly it was too bright in the room. He was smiling that pearly white smile of his.

"It was all right."

"Have any more fun with the ladies after I saw you last?"

"No, just drank and watched."

"I was with three," he boasted.

"Good for you," I said and regretted it.

I opened the top drawer and pulled out a pair of grey boxer shorts and a pair of equally grey socks. Next I opened the third drawer down and removed a white polo shirt, like a real tennis pro. I closed both drawers simultaneously, using my hip and leg.

"You mind?" I said, signalling with my boxers that I wanted to dress.

"No secrets here," he sniggered, then made a noise faintly resembling a car engine, which may or may not have been "Sure", before turning to face the window behind the bed.

I slipped the boxers on under the towel. I was shy like that; no guy had ever – or would ever – see me naked. I removed the towel and put the polo shirt on. Its material felt comfortingly soft as it pressed against my skin.

He sensed I'd finished or saw I had in a reflection in the window and turned back to face me. I opened the wardrobe, which stood next to the chest of drawers, and removed a pair of black Levi's.

As I pulled them up, he continued speaking. "Do tell, what's up?" I didn't answer immediately. Hesitation, he viewed, as a sign of weakness. Sensing my apprehension, he spoke again. "That guy last night, that was nothing, you know that."

"Not to me." I could only shake my head.

"Why, last night, I could've sworn you got a kick out of it." He got up and walked towards me, exuding confidence. "Hindsight's an incredibly useless thing, Sean. Like a wild animal, you were. Hell, you even scared me, and I don't scare easily. You telling me you didn't get a crazy rush out of giving that motherfucker what he deserved?"

"Whatever he deserved, there was no rush, not by a long shot. It's in my head all the time, Jimmy, and I can't get it out."

"Don't be soft, Sean. It's business, you know. Look at it from that angle and it won't seem so bad. First one's always the most difficult anyway and you handled yourself perfectly. You see, buddy, we do what we gotta do."

"And did I have to do that? Did I have a choice?"

He smiled. "Depends on how you look at it, I suppose."

"Never again, Jimmy." I shook my head. "Please. I can't be like that again."

"You're good at it, Sean. Why run away from what you're made for?"

"I'm not made for it. Not any more." Then I was louder. "I've fucking changed."

He didn't move, but his eyes narrowed. *What have I done?* I thought. I'd never raised my voice to him. Everything I had was because of him. I owed him so much.

He broke the silence with a snigger. "See that temper of yours, Sean, it's a valuable tool. People'll pay a lot of money for a temper like that. So why waste it? Use it, and let's make a fuck load of money together. What can you possibly be afraid of?"

I locked eyes with him. "Myself. I'm afraid of being like I was before."

He nodded. And he smiled some more.

"What the hell," I said, and that was when I told him – not every detail, but a good deal – about Jodie and my time with the Andersons.

He appeared to be almost impressed as he heard my tale, his eyes fixed intently on mine. He nodded occasionally, that was all, usually at the parts that made me wince the most.

"But don't you see? I don't want to be like that now. I'm different. Before Jodie and after, there were other things. Worse things." He gave me a glance that said, *I can believe that.* "They're in my head when I'm awake, when I sleep. They won't leave me alone."

"So use them. Take that frustration out on those who deserve it, and let's make loads of money."

"Jimmy, please. I can't take it any more. I want them to go away. And last night kicked everything even further down a hole. It's too much for me."

I waited for his response. For the whole time I'd been speaking, he hadn't interrupted me once. He knew when to speak and when to keep quiet, usually for his benefit.

"So you want out?" he asked.

"No, Jimmy," I jumped in quickly. "You've given me everything I've got. I owe you my life, and I always will. Remember that, I'll forever be in your debt. But, please, right now, can we keep things the way they were before last night?"

"I'll give you some time, Sean. Until you're ready. But I know you'll come around. People like you always do. It's inside you, deep in your soul. You can't hide forever."

"I can. And I will."

"Prove me I'm wrong. Go ahead and try. But I think we'll see that side of you again pretty soon. It'll claw its way back out. And when it does I'll be here ready and waiting to use you. Hey, if I'm wrong I'm wrong, but I don't think so." He made his way to the door. "You know what you got on today?"

"Couple of regulars," I answered. "Pretty flexible after that."

"Keep 'em happy, Sean. Keep 'em happy and they keep coming back."

I watched him walk away, casually, that same confident swagger as before. But in his face I recognised a touch of disappointment. He couldn't hide it so well.

Do it or don't do it, nothing could hide the fact that I needed Jimmy. Still.

Before

The police picked me up. I was a state. My life was a state.

The police, the cell, the doctor, the rehab. It was an easy-to-follow six months. At nineteen, I'd done it all.

"You can beat it. We can beat it. You can beat it." Doctors are nothing if not optimistic. I wondered if they believed the words they came out with. I think so. They have a view on humanity that won't falter: everyone can change; everyone is good deep down.

We talked every day. They asked me about my life. They asked me about my feelings. They asked me about my past – not that I could remember that much of it – and they asked me about my hopes for the future.

I talked about the guys I'd been with. I spoke of why I'd done it. There was no pleasure in it. It wasn't about desire; it was only about necessity. We need, we do. And I needed to live. But what kind of life had I given myself?

We talked about my parents. I was honest. I wondered if they were dead yet, and I longed for it to be true. I went through what he'd done to me again. I talked about the pain. Then the numbness. Then I talked about the tears. Then the dryness. I talked about the life I had, and the life I left behind for it. Neither one amounted to much.

He asked me what I'd say to my dad if he was ever in front of me again. I'd talk about hate, I said. The hate I had towards the man that was overwhelming. That would never disappear. I felt I could kill.

And I talked about what haunted me. My dreams. So many times I'd had the same dream. In it he'd found me. He'd punish me for leaving home. My mother wasn't there, not that that would bother him. He'd slap me. He'd choke me. He'd grab me by the hair, tug my head back and plant his teeth on my neck. He'd push me to the floor. He'd not speak once. His anger would come out through his actions. He'd get on top of me. He'd tear my shirt open. He'd yank my jeans off. I'd never have underwear on, like I was inviting him. He'd pull out his hard cock. I'd wince at the sight of it again. In the years I'd been gone it hadn't changed. And every time I'd be able to cry. I'd actually cry, cry like my face was pissing itself. And he'd push hard. My father would fuck me. And I'd sob.

I never woke up until he'd come. Until he'd bitten me again, drawing blood, and it poured from my neck. Until he'd won.

We talked of my dreams. Dreams that haunted me. Fucking nightmares, I call them.

Weeks Later

Believe in what you're doing and it won't seem so bad.

Jimmy said that to me not long after my birthday.

I tried to live by that philosophy during the following weeks. So, basically, I attempted to kid myself, for I knew it was nonsense. But the mind is powerful, so I got on.

During an alcohol-fuelled discussion, one of Jimmy's clients or partners or women, or maybe just a stranger he'd met in the street, let him in on a secret. The value of regular pharmaceuticals.

With this new-found knowledge, Jimmy set about organising what to do at the speed of a panther. Everyone was briefed and in place within the week.

The plan was simple. We went to a small town some fifteen miles from home and aimed to take down three chemists in rapid succession, then return home for dinner. And a celebratory drink, of course. Apparently the drugs – and here I mean legal prescription drugs – were big sellers. As a result, Jimmy wanted a hand in the game. He had the manpower and he had the nerve. He knew chemists weren't well protected against theft and we could easily get by a couple of security cameras at most. *Hit hard and hit fast.* There was the possibility of encountering one or two customers and, most probably, some female assistants, but nothing that would be a test. Jimmy assured us we could handle it. You just had to show them you meant business.

And he was right. That was the thing about Jimmy. Not only did he exude confidence, but he could carry off the goods. If he said we'd manage something we managed it without question. His confidence was at times infectious.

Three chemists, two miles at most separating each, and fifteen minutes spare between each job. No more than three minutes in each place. Grab all the merchandise you can fit into a sports bag. Our instructions were simple. Six of us meant lots of merchandise; lots of merchandise meant lots of rewards.

That was the plan and that was how we executed it. It came off slickly. Jimmy was delighted – he'd hit the new market with a stinging bang – and he immediately got planning on several more batches. In threes, for three minutes at a time. A simple yet effective plan, one we repeated six times over the next two weeks or so, until Jimmy was well stocked and able to meet demand. For demand was huge.

And then, just like that, he stopped us. He called a meeting nineteen days after our first job of three was pulled off and said *no more*. Not for now anyway. Police presence had increased since we'd begun – and probably as a result of us – and people were on their guard. He was equipped with all he needed for now.

We stop, he said, *and we start up again when we need to*.

Jimmy was like that. He was smart. He understood limits – he lived by them – and he wasn't greedy. In this game it was easy to become greedy, to want more, more, more, to push your luck and fall into a trap. To fuck it up. I saw a number of his guys heading that way and he shot them down. It was too dangerous, and clouded judgement. To deal, to make money, to evade the threats, for there were many, one had to see clearly; money couldn't get in the way, even when everyone's final objective was to make money and lots of it.

Money wasn't bad for me. I continued to earn my commission, my client list grew as people began to trust me and my work didn't involve beating the hell out of anyone, although Jimmy still revelled in that frequently. I sensed he was making too many enemies and dangerous friends and I worried for him.

A Friday night, normally a busy night, I returned home at about eleven thirty after things had got unusually quiet. Jimmy told me he'd planned on being home – the ladies were coming over. He wasn't there.

I returned my collection of pills, powders and substances, an A to Z of disintegration, to a compartment built into the back of the chest of drawers and sealed it shut.

On the way home I'd stopped off in a corner shop for a bag of popcorn. I tore it open and dropped it onto the bed. A few random pieces fell onto the duvet. I picked them up and chucked them into my mouth with a flick of the wrist. I undid the buttons of my shirt, took it off and draped it over the computer desk swivel chair. I went over to my DVD collection – eight films – and picked out the only film I hadn't yet watched. I removed it from its plastic case, scanned the front cover for a moment for the fifth time over the past week, and placed the disc into the player. *Sony*, real nice.

I jumped onto the bed and felt the relief that stretches over your entire body when you put your feet up after using them for a long period. I grabbed the popcorn bag, sighed and settled back for a relaxing evening.

The slamming of the bedroom door woke me with a start. I'd started to drift off to sleep. I instantly sprang up. Through the sleep in my eyes I made Jimmy out leaning against the wall. As the seconds passed and I saw more clearly, I recognised the familiar sight of blood. It ran down his check from under his left eye. The eye was already swollen shut and his lip was busted. I heaved myself off the bed, wide awake and, taking hold of him by the waist, led him to it. He supported himself by holding my shoulder with his arm and he limped as we stumbled forwards.

I hadn't a clue what to do and say but settled on, "What happened?"

"It's okay," he answered. His breathing was heavy. His left arm caressed his ribs. "Motherfuckers," he said to himself under his breath. He struggled through every syllable.

"Who Jimmy? Are you all right?"

"Do I look all right? Give me a hand here." I helped him lie down. "Get me a wet cloth, would you?"

I ran into the bathroom and quickly soaked a flannel. I grabbed a roll of toilet paper and went back to him. He was lying on his back as I'd left him, his teeth gritted and his fists clenched, and I could still make out his pounding chest. I tried to press the flannel against his cheek, but he snatched it from me and looked put out that I'd even tried.

"Now," he said, "go downstairs and get me some ice."

After I'd got the ice and returned to see him settled, I sat with him, choosing to place myself on the end of the bed.

"Good film?" he asked.

"No idea. Just woke up."

"And not in time to see the end. Fucking thoughtless of me."

I laughed. I thought it might help. It didn't.

I tried again. "What happened to you?"

"Drugs, Sean. You know how easy it is to piss someone off?" He clicked his fingers. "As easy as that. It's a dangerous game."

"Must have really pissed them off for them to do all that to you."

"Not the first time. Definitely ain't gonna be the last."

"And that doesn't frighten you?"

"Fuck, no. I do it every day."

"Why don't you stop, Jimmy?"

"Stop?" he repeated with a reign of sarcasm sifting through his voice. "I stop, how do you work? I stop, what about the other guys?"

"You don't do it for us, Jimmy."

"All right then. What about me? I stop, I got nothing. What do *I* do? With this, I've got something. This makes me important."

"Yeah, and a black eye."

"Since when did you become so fucking funny, comedian?"

"I worry for you, Jimmy."

"I don't need your fucking worry, kid."

I stopped.

"Can't please everyone, Sean. Gonna step on people's toes sometimes. If you wanna get to the top."

"But no one messes with you."

"What the fuck do you know anyway?" he snapped. "Fucking kid and you see, but you don't know shit. This is what it takes. You got it – I seen that and I know. You can give it, but you're so chicken shit, you're too scared to. Well, I give it and I take it. People mess. Deal with it. But tomorrow I'll get up and give it back twice as bad. And then it'll start all over again. The same people or somebody new. But, whatever, I'll fuck them up more than they'll fuck me up. That's the way it's gotta be."

I couldn't help but argue. "That's wrong, surely. There's got to be room for-"

"What? Room for every drug dealer? Oh yeah, come on. Let's share the playground like one big happy family. You must be joking." He spat out a snigger. "Like I said, kid, what the fuck do you know?"

I felt so small, like never before with Jimmy. I think I stopped liking him. I was trying to help. I couldn't understand his life or what he was saying. There had to be another way. But Jimmy hurt people for a living too. How long before someone actually fought back, before he got caught up with someone who wasn't scared?

He broke the silence. "Give me some space. Take a hike."

Without a word I left and closed the door behind me. I didn't look back.

I went into Jimmy's room, lay on his bed and shut my eyes.

One thought reigned over me: *I want out.*

Months Later

I just wanted a normal life, but my life wasn't normal, not by any stretch of the imagination. My days felt increasingly wrong. I spent more of my free time on my own and kept away from Jimmy, unless we had to discuss business. He too was more distant and that suited me fine. At times, he was merely the guy who slept in the next room.

I started going to the cinema on my own, for I didn't want to associate with anyone connected to drugs and they were the only kind of people I ever met. I went shopping and to a couple of pubs and clubs, daunting at first. There I got talking to a few people who I presumed led normal lives. And always the same question arose without fail: *So what do you do?* In return I'd deliver a well-rehearsed answer: how I worked in a factory and had been there for almost a year now.

I visited the library as well and reinvigorated my love of reading. I'd neglected it for too long. I felt comfortable there. I took books home on a weekly basis and, when I had time to take a seat, I always found something to pick off the shelf and spend a couple of hours reading. At their most regular, my visits were daily. Between deals I'd enter worlds even stranger than my own.

In all, I found ways to start enjoying life.

I had the afternoon free and I was in the town centre wandering round the shops, scouring shop windows for something attractive, when I spotted a job advertisement. An assistant in a woman's maternity clothing shop was needed for sixteen hours a week – not for me, I know, but it got me thinking. So I started moving from shop to shop, hoping that something might fit. *What would Jimmy say if you got another job?* I imagined the conversation we'd have and the threats of *I'm not gonna let you go, you know too much* that he'd have to employ, but I pressed on nonetheless.

The search resulted in nothing when, just as I was about to call it a day and head home, I noticed a sign for the local Job Centre. A sign, but no sign of the building. I followed the direction of the arrow on the sign along a path that ran between two buildings. Their brick shells had been heavily graffitied over. Letters, symbols, a dictionary of curse words and obscene diagrams stared you in the face.

The path veered to the right and later opened up into a small courtyard. Overwhelming – both in sight and smell – wheel bins had been deposited next to three of the four surrounding walls. Weeds peered through gaps in the cracked paving stones and yet more graffiti dominated.

Despite all the distractions, I spotted it. Three storeys high, its windows were covered in mildew and it was constructed of the dullest grey concrete you've ever seen, on which the faded yellow and blue sign announced that the Job Centre stood before me. A double door, brown in colour but peeling heavily, hung below the sign.

Like a gun firing, a woman, probably in her mid-twenties, barged through the stiff doors using her shoulder. Her eyes were crossed and she raved a collection of words under her breath. I heard the word *fuck* repeatedly.

I don't know what made me do it or why I asked such an obvious and stupid question, but when she was beside me I spoke to her. "Excuse me. Is this the Job Centre?"

She stopped in her tracks and said, "What the sign says, I guess so." She looked at me as though I'd been drinking and pulled a face. "Fuckers'll do fuck all to help you anyway." She turned back to the building and screamed, "What the fuck are you doing with my fucking life?" and bent forwards, her hands on her knees. I caught my first glimpse of her rear. The urge to jump behind her pulsated through my body. My palms sweated over. Then, not giving me a moment longer, she straightened up and stormed off, but not without leaving me with another opportunity to admire her body from behind.

100

I refocused and got inside. It smelt like a hospital, that vacant, sterile, almost death-like odour that clutches hold of you in its vice grip and doesn't let go, not until you leave or it's meal time when another bad smell takes its place. Immediately before me was a staircase that spiralled up and escaped from view. On the walls were posters that declared how much help was on offer here. Banal statements like *Want a job? We've got hundreds* tried to encourage punters but ultimately failed. I took them with a pinch of salt, bearing in mind the woman's reaction outside.

When I reached the top of the staircase, I came to a door with one full-length pane of glass in it and, again, pieces of paper informed me about how much help I could receive from within. Behind it I could see a vast office space, all grey, and a far improvement on the exterior. Supporting pillars were scattered asymmetrically to hold those upstairs up and rows of desks lined the near and far sides of the room. I entered. No one looked up and acknowledged me. The space was large and I felt incredibly small. A few other people were milling around. I needed someone's help to show me where to go. I was tempted to walk out but something, a faint glimmer of hope perhaps, kept me there.

Several employees, mostly women, sat behind the desks. At least two pairs of them were talking, making small chitchat from one desk to another, unconcerned that they had jobs to do. Resisting the urge to back off and get out of there, I proceeded further into the room. Still no one saw me. In the centre of the room next to the pillars were three separate machines – *Computer Job Search*, the notices above and on them declared – so I took solace by reaching for the closest one. I tried it out, but it didn't make sense to me. Feeling confused, I followed the on-screen instructions – age, area where you live, kind of work you're after – only to be asked for a password at the final stage. I looked for assistance, but those behind the desks were still in deep conversation.

I moved towards one of the women's desks. No response from her, so I moved closer. I was only a few feet away from the desk now, shuffling on my feet like a naughty schoolboy awaiting the stern headmistress's scolding and punishment, but nothing came from the woman who chatted so gaily. Was I invisible? I made a noise as if clearing my throat. I made it again. And again when, finally, the woman, who wore a big ball of a hairdo and spectacles so unsuitable they made her look like Miss Moneypenny on a very bad day, lifted her eyes, gave me a disapproving glare, turned away and resumed her chatter.

"Excuse me," I said, raising my voice and enunciating each syllable.

That got her attention. Hairball jolted to position and appeared flustered. She arranged some papers on her desk.

"What have I got to do to get some help here?"

She stood up quite unexpectedly and said in a whisper, "You will lower your voice, Sir, or you will leave at once."

"I've been waiting for your help since I came in," I protested.

"You will lower –"

"Who the fuck do you think you are, you stupid cow?" I shouted even louder, enraged at her now, and I heard my voice echoing the woman's outside. I leapt towards her desk until my leg connected with the wood, with my arm in the air.

She shrieked and shrunk back into her chair. It almost engulfed her.

I stopped myself. Much as I wanted to level the bitch I stopped myself.

I backed up and got out, brushing past those who'd come to assist her. No one came to assist me.

Jimmy or nothing. My options were simple. I chose Jimmy.

*

When I arrived back home, Jimmy was waiting for me in my room.

"Sit down," he said.

I sat.

"Where you been?"

102

"Shops."

"And?"

"Shops and shops."

"Anything?"

"Nope."

"Listen, Sean. Something important's happening on Monday and next week." My soul instantly shrunk. "Well, two things, actually. So I need your help. And it's not with beating some guy up. Unless you've changed your mind, that is. I got this big job to do. Gonna take time too, so I'll be away a bit. Thing is, my little sister Sarah is coming home at the same time. She'll be here on Monday for a week. Because you're a good guy I trust you. So I want you to take care of her while she's here. See, people don't like me, Sean. They see me as a threat. She can't be caught up in this, get it? And she can't know about any of what's going on around here. So next week you're off the drug beat and you're gonna look after my little sister. Take good care of her. Guard her with you life."

Day One

Like a thunderbolt had struck my heart, I felt it.

Have you ever been in a moment you knew would alter the rest of your life? Meeting Sarah was my moment.

Deep blue eyes, shiny blond hair, visible cheekbones and a smile that could infect the saddest of hearts welcomed me as she walked into the room for the first time. Jimmy introduced us. She had a bag on her shoulder and her hand was outstretched, reaching for mine. I took it. It was soft and gentle, and the very touch alone sent my insides squirming and my knees buckling.

"Nice to meet you, Sean," she said.

Her voice rang sweetly in my ears. Her former English accent was less obvious, touched by her newer life. Partly influenced by the American, it was a mixture of both and not entirely either.

"Hi."

I still had hold of her tender hand and something stopped me from letting go.

"God," Jimmy belched to get me off his sister. He pushed between us, separating our hands, and said, "Shall we go in?"

I clumsily stumbled backwards to make way for Sarah to pass. She gave me a smile and went to her bedroom, which was still set up from her last time here. She didn't need to be shown. I watched her walk by and disappear from view. She wore her hair long. It moved gently as if assisted by the coolest of breezes. She had a pink wrap around her neck. It looked like silk. She had on a light brown cotton top with full-length sleeves and a three-quarter length skirt. It was light grey. I could see the lower half of her tanned, toned legs. Her shoes were black and elegant, the toes covered and the heel open. I was mesmerised by her beauty, her elegance, her pleasantness. It was a feeling I'd never experienced before.

Jimmy looked at me, or the sick puppy before him. "Oh, please," he growled and left me standing there alone.

My body was limp, all my energy had been sapped and a heavy weight was pulling at the strings of my heart. A picture of her was perfectly visible in my mind's eye. It was a picture that could never improve, alter or leave. I desperately wanted to go to her room and ask her a thousand questions. She was like a magnet, her force tugging at me all the while.

I had no idea then, but in hindsight I realise that sex didn't cross my mind, even though she was incredibly sexy. Despite her beauty, my thoughts didn't take their usual route. Instead, I wanted beyond want to hold her, to talk to her, to touch her delicate skin, to kiss her. I wanted to explore her mind. I wanted to be with her.

*

Mere moments dragged on when I wasn't with Sarah.

That first day, for the remainder of the afternoon and the evening, she said she wanted to stay at home and rest. I had no idea what jetlag was like, but I hoped resting at home meant time to be together. I longed to get to know her.

Initially, it didn't. Sarah stayed in her room. I checked on her from time to time – as often as I could without seeming pathetic – and offered her a drink, a cup of tea maybe, or some crisps. Her usual answer was a thanks-filled rejection, until my fifth attempt when, later that evening, I knocked on her bedroom door and she called me in.

"Would you like a sandwich, Sarah?" I asked as I peered around the door.

"Oh, no, thank you. I don't want to put you to any trouble."

"It wouldn't be any trouble. None at all. I was just about to make one for myself. So no trouble. None."

She giggled at me. I secretly cringed at myself.

"Okay," she answered. "Thanks. That'd be great."

"I'll be right back," I said eagerly, and headed away.

With my head out of view, I charged downstairs like a bat out of hell – or heaven now – delighted by her response, excited to make her a sandwich, and hardly able to contain my smile. Gathering ingredients that would have made the greatest of connoisseurs jealous, I made the most perfect sandwich imaginable. Ham, cheese, lettuce, cucumber and tomato, with mayonnaise. That it took me three attempts is irrelevant; I got there in the end.

On a tray I placed a small crystal vase, filled it with water, and put a tulip from the kitchen table centrepiece in it. Joining the vase on the tray were the sandwich on a china plate, a glass of orange juice and a napkin. I picked the tray up and made my way out of the kitchen. Almost whistling, I tackled the staircase and arrived once more at her door. I knocked.

"Come in, Sean."

I went in. She was speaking as I did so. "Really, you don't need to knock." She saw the tray in my hands and sat up. "Oh, Sean, you really shouldn't have. That's beautiful. Thank you."

I loved the way she said *thank you* – the *a* was partially extended.

I put the tray down on the bed in front of her. She picked the vase up and sniffed the tulip. She smiled at me. "Thank you," she repeated.

"Don't mention it." I smiled.

"Okay. So where's yours? Are you not joining me?"

"I… um… Oh, it's downstairs. I didn't think…" and I trailed off.

She helped me out. "So go get it."

I smiled, laughed, almost killed myself with embarrassment, then almost killed myself by stampeding down the stairs. At the bottom, I tripped on the rug and fell to my knees. My hands partially cushioned the landing, but it still stung. The adrenalin was flowing, so I got up and whipped a sandwich together in seconds. No, it had nothing on the one I'd made for her.

In no time I was back. And out of breath. She hadn't touched her sandwich. She was waiting for me.

"What was that noise?" she asked me.

"What noise?"

"Like a loud thud." She gestured with her hand. "Sit down."

I sat opposite her and my prayer had been answered. We both crossed our legs and placed our plates before us. I think they were touching.

"It was nothing," I said. "I tripped. It's nothing. That's all."

Could I even put a sentence together?

"Are you all right?"

"It's nothing. Sure. Absolutely. Thanks."

My heart was racing and she giggled again. Such a soft giggle. She was aglow.

"Do I make you nervous?" she said shyly, her eyes slightly lowered.

"Kind of."

I couldn't believe it. I couldn't believe I said it. What kind of fool? There was something about her that prevented anything other than the truth from exiting my mouth. And now what would she think of me? Some kind of pathetic loser.

"Kind of?"

I paused. "I guess so." I hesitated again, momentarily, before it came out. "I've never known someone so beautiful."

Her eyes opened wide. I could tell she was surprised. I bowed my head shamefully. "Stop it," she said, modestly. "You don't mean that."

"Don't I?" I bowed my head even lower. I think my skin had turned bright red by now.

She saw my reaction and whispered, "My god, you really mean that?"

I started to get up to leave, but she stopped me by softly placing her hand on my wrist. "Please. Don't go. I'm sorry. I shouldn't have said that. I didn't want to embarrass you."

"Try humiliate," I said.

A pause, then we both smiled at one another.

"Please stay."

I'd never have refused in a million years, so I relaxed back onto the bed and picked my sandwich up. I took a bite, but only a small one from fear of having food dangling from my chin.

"Thank you," she said. To help me out she asked, "So, tell me, how'd you meet Jimmy? He didn't tell me much about you."

"He helped me out at a time I needed it most. I don't know where I'd be without him. I didn't have a home and he provided one for me. He's a good guy."

"Yes, he is. And a good judge of character too. He must've seen something special in you, Sean. Besides, he's got a heart. People don't often see it, but it's there. And I guess you're proof of that. I don't like what he does, Sean, not at all. I'm dead against it in fact. But he's a good guy. I do worry about him. He's gotta stop these things he's into."

"You know about that stuff?"

"Of course I do. He can't hide it from me, even if he tries and fools himself into believing he does. I've been back here enough to see it. And there's always someone like you – one of his guys – to take care of me. He likes to pretend I haven't got a clue, but I hear things. I just don't want him to get hurt."

"Your brother knows how to take care of himself, Sarah. Believe me, you don't need to worry about him." I fought valiantly to reassure her and prevent any apprehension from creeping into my voice.

"I hope you're right."

"Don't worry." I put my hand on her knee. "It'll be all right."

She had an incredibly thoughtful, calming air about her. I didn't want her to be upset, yet I feared the more she knew about me the worse she might feel. I changed the topic in an attempt to bring the conversation to a brighter tier.

"Jimmy's never told me about your life in America. Please tell me. Why did you move out there?"

"I've been there since I was nine. My dad has a younger sister out there, Aunt Vanessa. The complete opposite of him. She's so caring and loves kids. Anyway, she used to visit a lot; felt she had to because she knew how neglectful my parents were. Still are. You know, they haven't even come home to see me. They haven't seen me for ten months and they couldn't care less." A few tears welled up in her eyes. I hadn't removed my hand from her knee. She hadn't objected. I squeezed it harder. "It's okay, Sean. Anyway, as soon as I was old enough, I asked my aunt – begged her really – to take me with her to the States and get me away from here. Jimmy, though, he wouldn't dream of leaving. England's so his home. Now America's mine. When I saw where there was love, I went to it.

"So we live in a quiet, peaceful town called Fullerton. It's in California, near Los Angeles, so not far from a big city if ever you want the crowds. I live with my aunt, her husband Greg and their young daughter Ellie. They couldn't have kids of their own, so they adopted her about a year before I arrived. She doesn't know the truth, of course, but she's so happy. A beautiful little girl. She's seven. And she's my goddaughter."

She took the first bite of her sandwich and made an agreeable humming sound.

"Would you ever dream of coming back?" I asked.

"To this?" She meant her family, it was obvious. "Never to this. No. But I miss things about being here. So I guess, yeah, for the right reason, I could come back, one day. But my parents aren't the right reason, that's for sure. They've already shown me that today. They haven't changed and I doubt they ever will."

I nodded my head. "Life out there sounds great."

"I have love, Sean, you know what I mean? It's what everyone wants. And I think it's what every kid needs. If they don't get it they can't be the same, not ever. I've got a family that makes me feel special and is special. I wanted that forever and for nine years I didn't have it – only from Jimmy. I know I only visit, but I try to give Steve what Jimmy gave me. I try to make him feel better."

"I'd like to have something like that," I interjected. "I almost had a proper family of my own, but I messed that up as well. I never knew my dad – or my mum, for that matter; I was taken from her when I was eight and even before that I don't have any memories worth having."

"I'm sorry," she said, and this time she placed her hand on my knee. Her touch was warm and comforting.

I smiled at her. "Nothing to be sorry about. Life is life. It takes you where it takes you, I suppose. An endless road that one day comes to an abrupt halt. After life, I guess that's when you can regret it. When you're judged. Now I've realised you can decide where life takes you. Good or bad, it's up to you which way you choose to go. Before... before I was... I don't know... I was just wrong. But I've changed now and for the first time I like it a lot better. Especially with you here tonight."

She giggled and I did too. Her giggle, much like her smile, was infectious.

"Thank you, Sean," she said, unexpectedly.

"For what?"

"For wanting to know and for being interested."

"How could I not be interested?"

If I'd been red before, now I exploded into an unimaginably deep blush. I'd never met anyone quite like her and I couldn't stop myself. I didn't want to lie to this girl. I wanted to share everything with her.

"You're sweet," she whispered into my ear, and then it happened. She kissed me on my cheek and I thought I was going to faint.

Woozy, the first words in my head came out. "And you are stunningly beautiful and kind."

We spoke at length about any and every topic that night. She told me about the States and I told her how I dreamed of going there one day. She even suggested I visit her. We talked about ourselves and our likes and dislikes. And we made plans for the week ahead. Sarah remembered and told me about many

110

places she wanted to share with me. Time flew by. I opened up. I connected with her, I knew, the lady of my dreams.

As we said good night, I was fulfilled like never before. It was almost three a.m. and the time for sleep had long passed, but I hadn't wanted to leave her and I'd sensed she hadn't wanted me to leave too. I kissed her on her cheek, took her hands in mine and kissed her other cheek. Her skin connected sensually with mine. She said, "I've had an amazing evening."

I said, "Thank you for everything." And I meant every word.

The utter joy that ran through my being mixed with a pang of sorrow as I realised that I could only be with Sarah for a week. I looked at her and looked human. I felt love.

"Good night," I said.

She smiled, but I thought I caught a glimpse of that same sorrow in her eyes.

*

She stares into my eyes. She smiles. She is happy and, in that knowledge, I am fulfilled.

We hold hands, palms outwards, and link our fingers. She whispers the sweetest words to me. I lean towards her ear and whisper my secrets to her. She giggles. And she smiles even more, fuller, more beautifully, if that's possible.

Our legs start moving to and fro. We're dancing. She comes closer to me, our hands drift down by our sides and she places her chin on my shoulder. She feels nothing but comfort in our compatible bodies and she tells me. We sway from side to side to hypnotic music played by angels holding pure white harps.

She moves her head and her eyes meet mine. Her lips reach for mine. We kiss and share the warmth in each other's bodies. A sensation of bliss spreads throughout my body and she tells me she's never been happier in her life.

*

At first, sleep stayed away from me. I'd too much to think about. But when it came it was deep and the most refreshing I'd ever had. I dreamt only of Sarah; of her beauty, of being with her and being happy together, of her love. Sweeter, more peaceful sleep never befell any other and that night I knew I'd been blessed.

I awoke early the next morning ready to see her. Hoping to see her. Longing to be with her. I dashed out of the bedroom and into the hallway to see if her bedroom door was open. I wanted to recognise signs of life stirring from within. I wanted to hear Sarah.

I was disappointed to find the door closed and no noise coming from within. But it was only seven in the morning; what did I expect? Nonetheless, I felt fresh. I didn't want to knock and disturb Sarah's sleep, so I went downstairs to prepare breakfast for her. I came round the staircase banister with a swing and, surprised, blissfully surprised, I met her there.

"Thought I'd treat you to a surprise breakfast," she said, her smile beaming.

I couldn't help but smile, smile, smile.

*

"I wanna show you some place special," Sarah told me.

We went by bus to the outskirts of the city, a journey I'd never taken before, to a place I didn't even know existed. While travelling we continued speaking about our lives, she more than me because my life had only been colourful in a very black way and I wanted to spare her those painful details.

But she asked me about my family – my mother especially. I only answered truthfully and told her what I remembered, nothing which was particularly pleasant, not that I recalled much. I think I'd subconsciously forced myself to forget the details of the drunkenness, the drugs, the men and the bruises, so discussing it again gave me a shock – brought it to the forefront again. As I spoke, Sarah looked on with utter focus, interested and hanging on to my words as if they meant more than they really did. When the positions were reversed, she told me

112

more about life Stateside. I even asked her to repeat some of the things she'd told me the night before. I wanted to hear her voice and know about her life. The very chimes of the words she produced sent vibrations raging around my body and I felt weak. It was the first sense of weakness I'd ever encountered that I wanted to keep.

"This is our stop," Sarah said as she stood up.

Likewise, I did the same. As I did so, the bus came to an abrupt halt and I was catapulted forwards. I clung on for dear life to the hand rail above a seat head and managed to regain my balance with only my pride damaged. Sarah giggled. *What the hell*, I thought, and giggled too. She took me by the hand and led me from the bus. We thanked the driver and changed from the pavement outside to a dirt path that led off into the countryside.

"This is going to play hell with your trousers," she said, jokingly.

"A shame."

She wore a pair of elegant white trousers, flared at the legs, which clung to her body perfectly. They showed off her shape but were modest at the same time. She wore a white T-shirt on which there were dark horizontal stripes, each separated by a few centimetres, on top of which a white cardigan was draped.

The day was glorious. The sun shone and heated the air just right. The grass was greener than green and the sky blue as the bluest sea. As we walked, we cast shadows side by side and hand in hand on the grass. She was such a picture, I admired her. And she carried it off so casually as if she couldn't – or her nature wouldn't allow her to – recognise her own beauty. Her steps were light and we bounded along gracefully. She encouraged my slight skipping by swinging her arm back and forth and taking mine with it. I wanted to take hold of her. I wanted to kiss her. The urge was extraordinarily strong.

"Where are you taking me?" I asked her, a little breathless.

"You'll see," she said. She was so happy. Her eyes said so. She told me.

I stopped her and let our eyes meet. "Me too," I told her.

The path led us into a field. To get there we'd squeezed through hedges, stepped over plants and climbed a fence.

"Almost there," she said.

I was excited. I wanted to see this special place. Words couldn't explain what she was doing to me. I had to tell her somehow.

We left the field and went into some woodland. Between a few trees, there it was: a scene of undeniable beauty. Before us, through an opening between some of the trees, was a lake. We emerged from behind the trees and stepped onto a veil of pebbles. On the lake were a couple of sailing boats. Birds swam nearby. The water was an exceptional blue, like I'd never seen and never dreamed could be seen in this country. In the background beyond the lake, there was a spread of wildlife – trees and plants of every colour and in patches so that you could make out a cloud of green and yellow and pink.

"It's beautiful," I said.

"Isn't it?" Her smile was as vast as the nature surrounding us.

"So beautiful. I'm here in such a beautiful place." I took her by both hands and brought my face inches from hers. "And with such a beautiful lady."

"You're a special guy, Sean. You're gonna make somebody real happy some day."

"I want to make you happy, Sarah."

She turned away from me and lifted her hand to her face. I heard her sniff.

"What's the matter, Sarah?" I asked.

"I... Oh, Sean."

She turned to me and I hugged her. She gripped me tightly and I felt closer to her than I'd ever felt to anyone in my whole life. I'm sure I hadn't come out of the womb with so deep a connection to my mother, before I knew what she was like and what she did to me.

I was so happy, yet a desperate sadness held me in its wake. I couldn't understand why.

She breathed deeply and said, "I don't want this day to end."

"Me neither. This is like the most amazing dream, Sarah, and you are my dream."

"But next week I'm going home, Sean."

"We shouldn't think about next week."

"But I am."

"Me too."

"I know we've only just met, Sean, but I feel something. You're a special guy. I know this is right."

"Even though you don't know me well?" I asked, surprised that she felt it too.

"Even though." She nodded her head as she spoke.

"Me too. I've never felt this way before. I don't know how to react. I don't know what's happening to me, but it's the best thing that's ever happened to me. You are that best thing."

A tear fell from her eye. It rolled down her cheek. She slowly brushed it aside with her wrist. Another tear followed and she repeated the same motion.

It felt right to cry. I'd cried before, but it was for a different reason, not a pain like this. But I didn't have to fight it. Tears wouldn't come, even if I'd wanted them to.

She pushed one final tear away, straightened her back and took me by the arms. "Let's have the time of our lives, Sean. Right now. This is gonna be the greatest time we've ever had."

"Yes. Yes, it will be."

"Come on." She squeezed my arm and kissed my cheek. I wanted another. "I wanna show you something."

"I thought this was it."

"No, there's more. You'll see."

She led me along the man-made pebble beach that surrounded the lake. Her balance on the pebbles, despite time away, was perfect; I stumbled and literally sank to my knees.

We made it though. I needed her hand all the way. She drew me away from the pebbles and towards some trees. I looked up to the top of the highest one. My head tilted back ninety degrees. The branches, as they reached out to one another, blocked out the sun.

"Look at this," Sarah said and released my hand. I wanted it back.

She leapt a couple of steps ahead and came to a halt next to the trunk of the biggest tree. "Still here," she said, I wondered whether to me or to the tree.

"What's that?" I asked.

"Here."

I came to her side and saw what she was pointing at. The initials *S.B.* had been carved into the bark.

"Every summer," she began to explain," I would come here and I loved it. It's so peaceful and beautiful. Like nothing else. When I was eight, I carved my initials into this tree." She touched it, ran her forefinger along its rough surface. "And it's still here. Each year after that, I chose another tree and carved my initials into them all."

She moved to another tree and showed me. Then a third tree. Without fail: *S.B.*

"There should be nine here altogether. I don't know why I did it. I come back every summer when I visit."

"It's not corny," I insisted. "It's special."

"So now it's the tenth year. A special one. Come with me."

I followed her several more trees deep into the woodland.

"This one," she said.

From her pocket she extracted a penknife and began carving.

"I started doing it with a sharp stone, but I grew up and now the big girl's got a knife." She laughed. "It's so much easier. How times change, hey."

"And your beauty only grows stronger."

"Stop it, Sean," she said, hitting me playfully.

"Never." It was impossible.

"Your turn," she exclaimed, and she came to me. "Carve your initials with mine. Next to each other. This is our place now."

Our place.

"After ten years." She nodded. "Our tradition." A huge smile spread across my face.

"Yes. Ours."

She stroked my back as I got to work on the tree. A little more tricky than I thought it would be, with a touch more pressure, the letters *S.M.* were soon there, by *S.B.*'s side.

She took a close look when I was done. "Perfect," she concluded.

We stood side by side admiring our handiwork. Total satisfaction filled every hole in my being, and there were a lot of holes. I judged she felt it too.

"You know, I never asked you your last name. What is it?"

"Monroe. I used Anderson for a while, the name of my last family, but officially it's Monroe. Can't help but think of Marilyn, huh?" I exhaled loudly. "Haven't used that one for a while. We all have them, names, but I never thought so much pain could come from the sound of one. Oh, Sarah, I've been void these past few years – for so long – but you've changed that just by being you."

"You've got a lot going for yourself, Sean."

"I've got nothing except you. I'm going to lose you in six days, Sarah. I can't take it."

The true meaning of those words struck me like a bolt of lightning. I broke down. In front of her. The tears did come, after what seemed like a century's absence. The boarder had indeed been crossed, the police line cut in half, the armour breeched. I was weak. And I was glad to be. I cried and Sarah looked at me for a second. She just looked. Then she clinched hold of me by the back of my neck and encouraged my head onto her shoulder. She didn't say words. She didn't have to. I knew she understood me for she felt it too. We were found, then suddenly lost. We were hope, then suddenly despair. We were happiness, then suddenly and unexpectedly sorrow.

"I love you, Sarah." My words may have come out muffled, but she knew. She understood what I'd said. She knew

117

because she tightened her grip of my neck, so I knew she knew. Her support was immense.

"You're my soul mate."

Her words, her smile, her very touch, infected my saddened heart and I felt better.

If only you could see me now.

Week One

Have you ever been stuck in time? When you don't want time to move on? When everything else is irrelevant? Nothing else matters. Only that moment. When it's there, it takes hold of you and your mind knows nothing else.

For me I was stuck in time in the best way. Utter happiness. After we'd carved our names onto the tree, the whole day fused together. I couldn't tell you how long it was. I could barely tell you where else we went for I was so transfixed by Sarah that I knew of only her and her words. When you meet like this, a warmth runs across you. Could Nine exists – I just never understood to what extent – and I was on it.

We returned home late that evening. The lights in the house were out. I unlocked the front door, held it open for Sarah and followed her in when she passed me. I was learning.

"I can't believe they still haven't come to see me," she told me as she placed her handbag on the stairs.

"Did Jimmy tell you where they are?"

"He left me a note this morning. Dad's at a conference, he said, and Mum's gone with him. She never does that. They could have at least made an effort."

"It's okay," I whispered. "I'll be with you."

I stepped behind her and softly massaged her shoulders. She had her hand on the telephone table, but her arm instantly relaxed. "Fantastic," she mouthed, separating the syllables as I rubbed her shoulder blades.

"All night if you like," I joked.

She turned around and faced me. Her eyes narrowed momentarily and suspiciously. Then she loosened her features and said, "Might just take you up on that. Watch what you offer. Your fingers'll be sorry." She laughed and I joined her.

"You want something?" she asked me.

"A drink would be great. I'll make them," I offered, but she was already there.

"I know. How about some wine?"

"All right."

She went over to the fridge and removed a bottle while I gathered two crystal glasses.

"White or pink?" she asked.

"You decide."

"White. This one's sweet. Sweet okay for you?"

"Perfect."

We took our drinks into her room. She put the stereo on and played some Toni Braxton. A beautiful song that only increased how utterly content I felt. We sipped on our wine and continued talking about life. I never believed I could find it so easy to speak to someone. I never believed I'd have so much to say and have this much pleasure from listening to another person. Sarah was impeccable company from the moment of waking to the moment sleep came. Charming, witty and heart-warming, she was perfect in a world in which I'd started to believe perfection didn't exist.

"What are your dreams, Sean?"

"You're asking me about dreams? The one without even a family of his own."

"Stop feeling sorry for yourself. I'm interested."

"You really want to know?"

"You know I do."

"My dream. I haven't thought about it before, but now it's simple. You've helped me realise it. I want happiness, Sarah. I want happiness in my life. With you. I want a life with you. It's that simple."

"But it's not so simple, Sean." She sighed and paused. Her eyes lowered to the duvet. Even at this stage, we were like mind-readers. I knew what she was thinking before she spoke. "Even though I wanted you to say something like that, the sound of the words chews at my heart."

Suddenly it was too painful to look at each other. What we were setting ourselves up for – the fall – was all that rang, and it rang deep.

With her eyes still fixed on the duvet, she broke the silence by saying, "I want to have a bath."

My heart caved in. I wanted to punch the wall, but I fought desperately to hide any signs from appearing on my face. Why had I said it? Why had I told her that dream? I hadn't wanted to scare her off. It was the truth and it had cut our evening short.

"I understand," I said, and rose to leave. "Thank you for–"

"Where are you going, Sean?"

"I'm sorry. Maybe I shouldn't have said something so full on. I'm sorry if I embarrassed you."

"Embarrassed me?" she laughed. "How did you embarrass me?"

"By what I said. I thought-"

"Stop it, you." She had a huge grin on her face. "You're such a worrier. Your dream is sweet. And mine isn't much different. I want to take a bath. But I want to take a bath with you, Sean."

What could I say? I simply nodded my head and smiled. I thought about it. *Bath. Together.* Bath meant naked. Naked meant showing Sarah my body. What if she didn't like what she saw? The first person I'd ever had the truest desire to give myself to and I was scared.

But it's your Sarah. Think about it.

I thought about it.

Then I said, "With me?"

"Yes, Sean. With *you.*" She got up from the bed and came to my side, took me by both shoulders and gently pressed them. "With you. Don't worry. Let me relax you."

"I'd like that."

She took me by the hand and led me from her room to the bathroom like a child being hurried along. The hallway corridor along which we walked seemed longer and darker than usual, but I thought I caught sight of a bright light at the end of it.

"Grab some towels, would you?" she said.

I opened the airing cupboard, choosing two towels – one pink with patterns on it and the other blue and plain. They smelt countryside fresh.

I got moving again and arrived at the bathroom door. Sarah had closed it. I paused for a moment to compose myself. Nervousness and excitement both filled me, a combination that never ceases to amaze me. First-night nerves. Competition final. An exam. It happens for so many reasons.

The sound of water falling into the bath was audible and I took that as my cue to enter. I pushed the door handle down, opened the door inwards and entered into the startling light. It engulfed me like a shadow of an aeroplane passing overhead on a sunny day. Sarah was leaning over the edge of the bath, checking the water with her hand as it fell into the tub. The water ran freely from the taps like it was desperate to escape from a hidden chamber, enter the safe passage of the bath and intoxicate our bodies with its warmth.

I stood in the doorway, unsure of what to do. Sarah wore only a black bra and white stringed underwear. I witnessed, in a different way from before, utter beauty, beyond comparison, a vision so complete, but I couldn't go closer. I didn't trust what I'd been. I was in fear of something wonderful. Her outline was rounded, her skin looked so smooth and her hair shined under the light. I wondered how it would feel if I were able to run my fingers along her delicate body.

My mind awoke from its wanderings when it was stirred back to reality by the sound of a familiar giggle. "Are you going to come in?"

Oh, I loved her voice.

I stepped further into the bathroom.

"And the door?" I looked behind me, unsure. "Could you close it?"

"Oh, right."

I closed the door and slid the lock quietly across.

Is there sweat on my head? I kept thinking. *Has she noticed how nervous I am?*

"Bubbles," she said, and she clapped her hands together before she reached for a bottle and softly squeezed its contents into the water. Steam was already rising from the bath; my temperature was rising at an equal pace. Sarah placed her hand back into the water after returning the bottle to the side of the bath and swayed her arm back and forth to encourage the bubbles to multiply. They did. She finished, stood upright and looked at me. Her face was so lively it inspired life in me. She shrugged her shoulders and walked to me.

"Let me help you," she said.

I wore a black shirt and navy-blue jeans. She slowly unbuttoned my shirt, one button teasingly at a time. It felt spectacular. The water on her hands had cooled, and touched my skin. The tips of her fingers and her nails occasionally rubbed against my chest. Goose bumps developed. She slid the shirt off my shoulders, caught it before it fell on the ground and placed it behind her on the towel rack. She ran her fingers down from the front of my neck, over my chest and stomach, finally to the buttons of my jeans. My breathing became heavier and there wasn't anything I could do to hide it. She took hold of my jeans and pulled the buttons apart. My heartbeat pounded at the inside wall of my chest. My lips were dry and I had difficulty swallowing. She went down onto her knees and eased my jeans to the ground, revealing me like a jack-in-the-box. I stepped out of the jeans and never once took my eyes away from hers.

She looked at me there. "Whoops." She smiled.

Inside I cringed, but she'd reassured me without knowing it and I no longer cared about feeling embarrassed. With her I felt safe and sure. I felt human. "You did it to me. It's your fault," I said in a whisper.

"No. It's my privilege."

She rose to her feet and pressed her lips against mine. Her luscious, tender touch. She took me by the hand and said, "Together, okay?"

"Okay."

"In three."

"In three."

"Three. Two. One."

We removed our own underwear on the sound of *one*. Our eyes stayed fixed on each other's. She lifted her hands behind her back and, without blinking from my line of vision, unclipped her bra. I saw her take a deeper breath than usual before she lowered it. Still her elegance reminded me of that of a swan gliding gracefully on the water.

For me this was my first time. For me this was the first time I'd seen a lady's body. The curves – pert, toned, perfectly proportioned – took my breath away. "Beautiful," I said.

She looked down at me. Maybe I blushed. "You too."

We smiled, relaxed finally, and stepped into an embrace. It was deeper than ever. At the same time, hand in hand and step by step, we got into the bath. I sat first and she sat herself between my legs with her back to my chest. Her shape from behind was mesmerising.

"Your hairs tickle my back a little." She shuffled in the water.

"Sorry," I said.

"I like it," and I felt relieved.

She rested her head back on my shoulder area. I leant back against the wall behind the bath and rested too. Like never before.

*

Candles burned brightly; their scents filled the room. We lay on the bed next to one another in our dressing gowns. My arm was placed around Sarah's shoulder and my hand gripped her arm. I never wanted to let go. Her head used my chest as a pillow and her hand held my stomach. Her touch was comfortingly warm. She could hear my heart beating and lipped its sound. It was beating for her. Her right leg was hooked around my ankle. We didn't speak. It wasn't necessary. We'd had the most romantic night of our lives and were filled with contentment, happy to know that tomorrow would bring with it another opportunity to create even more special memories for the future. And the time to fall deeper in love.

That night had been all about sharing emotions and developing a love so strong. Our evening had been erotic in every way. I learnt that eroticism is about feelings, not only about sex. Although I longed for Sarah, I longed for her as I had her: in my arms. The opportunity for sex was there, but neither of us mentioned it. We had everything we needed just by being together. We *had* given our bodies to each other that night, just in a different way.

Between Sarah and me, I now believed anything was possible. Love would lead us down its path and we'd follow it wherever it dreamed to take us.

Before

I managed eight months the first time. The cravings slowly went away. The pain was always there, but it wasn't as strong any more. These eight months weren't doing a damned thing to give me my life back. How can locking yourself away be anything similar to real life? I wanted real life, and real life meant being on the outside. Being free.

The day I took off, I hugged the doctor after our session. He'd helped me. I couldn't argue with that. And I'd cried again. That night was the time. I had to do it. Security wasn't tight; I wasn't a threat. So I walked out of the door. I headed into the street for the first time in eight months and I breathed the fresh air of the city. It was putrid but it was what I needed. Right or wrong, I was free.

Wrong.

That Night

Loud music, so many people dancing, making out and rubbing up against one another, smoke machines, flashing lights, and a flowing fountain of alcohol and cigarettes. Nightclubs had never really been my scene, but I can understand their attraction to the revellers who religiously attend every weekend.

Visage – incorrectly pronounced by those who owned it, those who worked there and those who partied there – was a popular nightclub in the heart of the city that attracted hundreds of youngsters seeking a fun time and a little added pleasure each day and more at the weekend. I'd been there on a few occasions before, usually with Jimmy when we had free reign of the place, and I'd always found it pleasant enough, so when Sarah asked me the take her there the following day I accepted without considering what the consequences could be.

After an enjoyable day, waking up late and lying in each other's arms longer, getting to know one another better, ice-skating – the first time I'd been in my life, meaning I spent most of the time on my backside and laughing while Sarah skated effortlessly around me – and having a romantic dinner by candlelight at a great Italian restaurant, we returned home, freshened up and headed out to Visage.

As soon as we passed through the reception area, the dance floor welcomed us with what appeared to be two arms open wide. We stepped between a set of blackened double doors. The dance floor had three levels: the balcony area on which we entered, except it was more like a floor all to itself, it was so vast in space; a pit, above which we stood, was the busiest place with hundreds of dancers, movers and shakers crammed shoulder to shoulder but somehow still managing to bob up and down to the repetitive beat of the music; and a raised tier, like a platform, to the back and slightly above the pit. I could see three staircases leading to it, one from each side of the balcony and one which came from the pit. Four bars surrounded the balcony area and there were several others on the floor below us. Lights of all colours flashed, spot-lit, illuminated and shone in every way possible.

Sarah's hand was in mine as I led her through the crowd. Party-goers danced on the spot and others chatted by screaming to be heard above the thumping music. Sweat poured off foreheads and soaked naked arms.

"What would you like?" I called to Sarah.

"Actually, can we skip the drink for a moment? I'd really love to dance with you first."

Dancing in public – actually dancing full stop – had never interested me. I always imagined the people around me watching, examining my moves and laughing.

"What the hell," I said to myself.

"What's that?"

"Sure thing. Let's go. You want to be down there?" and I pointed to the popular pit below.

"No, over there's good." She pointed to a space where people were dancing nearby but not in such huge wolf packs. Heavy metal concerts had nothing on the volume of music being played in here. Sarah shouted, "Too many people down there. I wanna be able to see you and dance with you, not half the city."

Now in charge she took my hand and led me through the ever-growing crowd. The songs – not that I could identify where one ended and the next began – that ricocheted off the walls had a thumping bass. I had no idea how to move my body to it, but judging by the people around us nobody else did either.

"Don't expect much from me." I had to repeat myself twice.

She eyed me inquisitively, then shrugged her shoulders while delivering another of her heart-stopping smiles. "Don't worry," she admitted. "Just have fun."

I wanted to hold her, to cradle her in my arms, while we danced, but the music didn't permit it. No Eric Clapton here. Her touch would have reassured me that I was doing all right.

But no such luck. Still, as often as I could, I held on to her arms and felt refreshed and reassured.

After several minutes I was comfortable dancing with her. I jokingly shook my backside and, realising what I'd done, avoided the drunken glances of those surrounding us, instead focusing on Sarah's laughter. She moved with grace just when I thought the music was telling me that was impossible. I was impressed.

The dance finished and we made our way back to the bar and ordered drinks. There was no way we'd find a table, so we made do with the shelf that ran along the entire side wall on which numerous couples had placed their drinks and by which they were stood deep in conversation or with their tongues down each other's throats.

Sarah and I talked; already we were discussing the times we'd had and the memories we'd built together. It was like we'd been together for ever.

A second dance and I was beginning to get the hang of it. Sarah was still all smiles. I'd never got dancing, but it had a way of making you feel exhilarated, that much I couldn't deny.

Couldn't deny.

I'm reaching for Sarah's hips and I feel it. A sharp pain, initially like a pin prick, which quickly feels like a cheese grater being dragged along my skin and, finally, a repetitive drumming pain on the back of my head. I'm unaware that I'm falling to the ground, but I realise it when I end up on the ground several feet away from Sarah. Three guys, all dressed in leather jackets, are surrounding her, pointing their fingers in her face. They're shouting, but I can't hear what they're saying. Can't even hear the music any more. Sarah's glance filters between them and me. But I'm on the ground and I can't get up. She has tears in her eyes and I can see she wants to get away from them. I try to get up but fail three times. I can't move. My vision is blurred. A high-pitched ringing, like a whistle being blown at half-time, builds up in my ears. The dizziness increases and I'm on my back.

If anyone apart from Sarah has paid the slightest attention to me, I can't tell. I see only the legs of the three guys as they move closer around her, surrounding her like hunt dogs, and I know I have to get up. I will it, but it doesn't happen. My hands sway from side to side before finally making contact with someone's leg. Using it, I pull myself up and manage to reach my knees.

One of the guys has Sarah by the chin. He's shouting at her. She's trying to get away, but one of the others has her around her wrists. I stagger to an upright position. I want to move in her direction, but all I manage is left and right. As I see a guy raising his fist, my hand reaches out. I manage to grab hold of a bottle. And all I know is that I leap. Leap in her direction. In their direction. As I begin tumbling forwards, back onto the ground, I swing the bottle. It smashes to pieces on the guy's arm. His grip of Sarah is released. As I hit the ground, I catch sight of him falling onto his knee.

Lots of attention around us now. Feet running away and my eyes close. Relief.

I don't remember much after that other than what Sarah told me later. We spent three hours in the A and E, what with the waiting time and the time it took for the stitches to be put in. Only five stitches, but the pain was so strong.

After the hospital, Sarah helped me home to bed. There I awoke the next morning, groggy and confused. Sarah sat on the edge of the bed, her eyes fixed on me.

"Hello, my man." I could sense she felt relieved to see me wake up.

My eyes adjusted to the light. Sarah's voice soothed me. "Good morning." My voice was hoarse. Sarah passed me a glass of water and I sipped on it after propping myself up on one elbow.

"You mean afternoon," she said.

The surprise of how long I'd slept hit me and I sat up with too much haste. Dizziness rained over me like a cold shower.

Sarah helped me back and said, "You took quite a bump, Sean. I'm so sorry."

"You did nothing, Sarah." She started to sob. "Please don't."

"It's my fault. They only did it 'cause you were with me. Why couldn't they have just waited for me to be alone?"

I managed to prop myself up on one elbow again. "What are you talking about, Sarah? Who are you talking about?"

"The guys last night. They hit you and threatened me. Told me I had to stop Jimmy from taking any more of their patch."

"Who?"

"Some dealers, I don't know."

I managed to sit and hugged her tightly. "Everything's fine. I promise. I'll never let anything like that happen again."

"But they hurt you. Because of me."

"Not because of you." I wiped a tear from her cheek. "Because of your brother." I looked her in the eye. "I will always be prepared now. You have my word."

"But what if they carry out their threats?"

"I'll speak to Jimmy."

"He won't listen, Sean." Her voice was louder than usual.

I said firmly, "Then I'll make him listen."

An uncomfortable silence filled the air. Had I threatened Jimmy? Was the same thought running through Sarah's mind?

I broke the silence. "Sarah, we've got to get out of here."

She sat on her knees. "I was thinking that too."

"You can't leave," I pleaded. "We can't be apart."

"Then come with me."

"To the States?"

"What the hell, yes. Come with me, Sean, and let's get away from all this."

I'd been derailed like a train. "But how? It's not possible. Jimmy."

"Tell him, Sean. Tell him and let's get out of here." She took my hand. Her warmth comforted me. "Start a new life with me."

I desperately wanted to yell *yes* and agree, but there were so many hurdles in our way.

"Nothing would be better, but I can't just leave." I thought deeply. "Can I?"

"There's nothing that can't be done. Of course you can. Come with me and keep me happy like now. You've got money saved, haven't you?"

"Yes."

"Then buy a return ticket but don't return. My aunt can sort the rest out when we're there. Just think, Sean. We could be together always."

"Happy for ever," the words etched across my lips and mind.

"Yes. For ever."

It came to me so quickly I don't think anything could have prepared me for it. Pain returned and I reached for the back of my head. My passport. I'd left it at the Andersons' house. I told Sarah.

"So let's go get it back then," she said.

"But I haven't told you everything about why I left." I sounded desperate. I had to tell her. "Sarah, I ran away. I made a stupid mistake – one of so many in my life already – and I hurt my foster sister. So I panicked and took off."

"We've no choice. You can make amends."

"I know we have no choice." There was only one way about this. "I wasn't a good person, Sarah. Truth be told, there isn't a word to describe what I was. I've got no excuses. But you healed me, and my time here also."

"You can make it all better."

"If only you knew, you'd want nothing to do with me."

She held me by the shoulders and faced me. "I'm not scared of you, Sean. I never will be. It's time to do the right thing."

"I have to apologise."

"That's right."

"I probably tore them apart. I'll go to them and I'll show them how I've changed. And I'll beg them to forgive me if I have to. I'm so sorry, Sarah."

She clasped her arms around me. "I know you are."

132

She released the hug and kissed me on the mouth. Her tongue felt like delicate fingers giving a massage.

"I need to tell Jimmy," I said.

"I know."

"And I need to do it alone."

Later That Night

"Who the fuck you think you're talking to?"

"You. You put your sister's life in danger."

"You've got a nerve, you ungrateful shit."

Jimmy was furious with me for speaking up. I'd seen this side of his temper before, like he'd seen mine, but it had never been directed at me.

"You're not listening to me," I protested. "Those guys whose patch you're moving in on, they threatened your sister."

"I put you there to look after her. Now you understand why."

"They went for her because of what you're doing."

He shrugged his shoulders. "Nature of the business."

"You can't possibly mean that." I was beginning to feel helpless. "You're not telling me you'd put drugs before your own family."

"And since when has my family ever put me first?"

"Fine, before your sister then. She cares about you. Sarah's not your parents, Jimmy. She only comes here for you and Steve."

"Fuck my parents."

"Three guys, Jimmy. She could've been hurt."

His eyes fixed on me. "But she wasn't."

"I was. Does that mean anything?"

"You get paid. I told you to look after her. You let your guard down, that's your problem."

"Your sister means a lot to me."

"Yeah, and to me too."

With emphasis: "No, *a lot*, Jimmy."

He sneered. "Touching."

"If you care about her like you say you do, act like it."

He froze and looked surprised. It was the first time I'd told him how to do something.

"Telling me what to do now? What next?"

"I just don't want Sarah to get hurt."

"And you think I do?" His eyes flitted about the room. "You come here, in my home, after all I've given you, after all I've done for you, and you tell *me* what to do. You get the fuck out."

My nerves twisted up. It couldn't end like this. "Jimmy, I didn't want to fight about this. But you've got to see how your business affects others."

"My business is doing just fine." He walked behind the sofa and leant against it. "The money you've got in your pocket is proof of that. Or have you already forgotten after only such a short time? You're one of those scummy drug-dealing piece of shits too and it saved you." He slapped his lap with both hands. "I fucking saved you."

"That's right. You did." I knew I had to sound confident here, so I tried my utmost. "But not any more. I'm not one of them any more."

"Meaning?" he asked, calmly.

"Meaning, I'm out."

He straightened his back and stood upright. "You're only out if I say you're out."

I held my ground. "I'm packing up my things and I'm leaving with Sarah."

"With Sarah?" His shoulders suddenly hunched forwards.

"We're going to the States together. I'm leaving, Jimmy."

"With Sarah?" He nodded his head. "And what exactly will you have with Sarah? Nothing. Drugs, Sean, they're your life now." I shook my head in protest. "You think not? I know. You don't know anything else. Why change a winning formula? We're a winning team."

"I want to be with Sarah."

"Sarah?" His shiny white teeth appeared again, only this time his smile was a mock grin. "You hardly know her. You'll be fed up with each other by the time you land and on to the next within a week."

"I know her better than you think," I said. "These past fours days I've been with her, I've never been happier and it's all because of her. We're going to be together."

"Pathetic," he sneered. "What, a nice piece of arse comes along and you change your ways?"

"You're talking about your sister, Jimmy. Can't you understand how love makes you feel?"

"I understand I've seen you cum with a strange woman rubbing herself on your cock. And you weren't thinking about love then, were you?"

"No." I shook my head. "Please. This is different."

"Someone like you doesn't know how to love, Sean. You're like me. I've seen deep inside of you."

"Not any more. I'm different."

"Wonder if little sis would like to hear about it then, if you're so different now."

I moved towards him and pleaded, "Don't. Please. You'll destroy us."

He went over to the window and looked out of it. The sun had disappeared and clouds had formed. He sniggered to himself. "Go then. Get out. Take your shit and leave."

I approached him. I had to make good. "Jimmy, you've helped me no end. That means a lot." I wanted this to be genuine. "Thank you."

He didn't turn around. "By walking out on me?"

"No, by moving on. We all do."

"I don't." His voice sounded regretful somehow.

After a few more seconds, he faced me. Without a hint of emotion, he said, "Now take your stuff and get the fuck out."

He brushed past me as he left the room, although I knew by now there was no real danger. I heard the front door click shut and he was gone.

Jimmy was gone from my life – and I was well and truly out of his.

*

Sarah, who'd been waiting outside in the garden for my conversation with Jimmy to end, came in about five minutes later. I was already packing a bag and preparing to leave.

"You all right?" she asked.

"Not the conversation I'd hoped for exactly. Still, I'm out. That was the result we wanted, wasn't it?"

"Yeah, he told me. Went on at me for a while, but Jimmy's so loose himself he'd never get in the way of something I wanted. You're lucky you wanna be with me and not someone else." She paused. "I asked him to come as well. To get out of here. Leave behind all the trouble he's in."

"And?"

"What do you think? He'll never give it up. I'm so worried about him."

I dropped the jumper I had in my hands and met her in the doorway.

"It's okay, baby. He knows how to look after himself."

"I've always wanted to love, Sean. My brother. And now you."

"And I will always be with you." I kissed her and stroked her shoulder. "Only you. Nothing will come between us doing this."

Sarah took three steps forwards, forcing me back. She closed the door behind her. In what seemed like slow motion she removed her blouse, revealing a black bra. She looked a little nervous but didn't say a word. Instead, she gently took my hands and placed them on her breasts. They were so soft to touch. She inched her lips to mine and we began to kiss. A slow pace, then more brisk, until we were kissing passionately. It was Sarah who moved me towards the bed. It was Sarah who removed my clothes and the remainder of her own. It was Sarah who sat astride me. She rocked delicately back and forth. Her breathing was deep and she made quiet sounds of pleasure. The heat from inside her warmed my heart, body and mind. I held her by the hips and moved my body in motion with hers. We were as one. I sat up and our chests connected. Our hearts beat together. I kept my eyes open the whole time. I needed to look into her eyes, to remind myself. For it was real. And I could see I was truly alive.

*

We lay under the duvet. My arm was around Sarah's upper back. She rested her head on my chest. We were tired and satisfied. We'd made love. My first time; perhaps hers too. We spoke of nothing and only rested in the contentment of what we'd just shared.

After some time, I filled the calm silence. "Thank you."

She reached further round my waist and gripped tightly. She smiled.

"My heart's come undone," she said. "I never let anyone in my heart before and now you're really there. And it's the best feeling."

"Thank you," I repeated.

"For what, Sean?"

"For letting me in."

We filled the final hours of the day in each other's arms, bathing together, eating and finishing our packing. Today was the start of the rest of our life together, but tomorrow would be a matter altogether different, I was quite sure of it.

Later Today

Blood on the wall gave it away. A teenage tryst, a tussle and lives changed for ever.

The Andersons returned home not twenty minutes after Sean had fled. They called upstairs to their daughter, but Jodie didn't answer. Nothing unusual there.

With the shopping unpacked some minutes later, Mrs Anderson headed upstairs to change.

"Jodie," she called as she mounted the staircase.

No answer, still hardly strange.

A pause as she neared the upstairs landing.

No, it couldn't be.

A closer look.

"What the hell?" A moment. "Jodie?" her voice full of alarm. "Jodie!"

Without knocking Mrs Anderson drove through Jodie's bedroom door. She gasped at what she saw.

Her daughter lay motionless on the bed, her eyes closed.

Mrs Anderson rushed to Jodie's side and grabbed her by the shoulders, frantically shaking her. "Jodie," she repeated. "Alan!" she cried at the top of her lungs.

Shocked, Jodie's eyes sprang open and she bolted to an upright. Blood had seeped through her top and covered her stomach.

"Cassandra," Mr Anderson called from outside the room as he approached. As his head came round the door, he asked, "Is that blood on the walls?"

He noticed his daughter.

"Bloody hell."

"Mum. Dad." Jodie tried to remain casual through the pain she felt.

"What happened?" they asked simultaneously.

Jodie looked down at her mid-section. She hadn't figured out what to tell her parents yet. She said, "I thought that was all a dream. It's fine. Really."

Mrs Anderson took a closer look. Sounds came out of her mouth, but they were not words. She squinted to focus on the skin, beyond the dried blood. She couldn't see clearly, but needless to say it was not fine.

With her mother bent double and examining her, and her father's angry eyes reddening, Jodie saw that her words needed to be more convincing. "I had an accident. That's all. Really, it's fine." She placed her arm shyly in the way to block the view. "It looks much worse than it is. I was going to clean off the blood, but I must've fallen asleep. Can we just forget about this?"

Ashamed – afraid – Jodie didn't want to reveal the extent of her sexual exploits to her parents, so she played the sweet, innocent girl once more, hoping it would all go away. Her parents, she thought, had no idea. And she was right to a degree. Ignorance is bliss and Jodie had been in, and managed to avoid, her fair share of trouble. She liked the wrong crowds – the cool guys, the unruly, promiscuous and undisciplined gonna-do-what-I-wanna-do gangs. Too young and too stupid, she listened to any older guy with a cute smile and a fast car. And she used her body, her pouting and her teasing to take control of any younger guy – one with a cute smile and the prospect of one day getting behind the wheel of a fast car. She'd been excluded from school twice before for adopting that gonna-do-what-I-wanna-do attitude and her parents, her dad especially, had come down hard on her. So much so they thought they had her under control. Little did they know the truth. She'd managed to avoid serious trouble with the police – usually because of fast feet – so the extent of her escapades was fairly under wraps. She'd shoplifted; she'd encouraged one of those cute, fast-car boys to assault another less fortunate; she'd enjoyed taking drugs; she'd even blown a stranger for cash and had come out of it with a big smile on her face. She'd bedded plenty of guys before – Sean was way down on the list. She craved the privacy, née parental ignorance, to enable her to have the time of her life.

This wasn't simply going to disappear, she knew that. Blood had given it all away. It had to be cleared up. With a form of the truth.

Her mother broke the silence and spoke softly; it was all she could muster. "Honey, tell us what happened. It's important you tell us."

"Please, it's fine." Jodie began to cry. *Will it work?* "Just let it go."

"I don't think we can. Not until you tell us, anyway."

"Please-"

"Speak now, child!" Her father's stern voice boomed. "Enough of this nonsense. Speak!" He barely moved a muscle but she was petrified.

With her head hanging down Jodie could think of only one way out. "To you," she whispered. "But only to you, Mum."

Her mother straightened up. "Give us some time, Jeff."

Jeff Anderson's lips pursed and his face reddened. He looked like a man on the edge, but he merely nodded and left the room.

Outside he stood above the stairs. He looked down at the bloodstains on the carpet, then on the wall. His head raised and his vision travelled, coming to a stop on the open door down the corridor: Sean's room. He stalked over to it and looked inside.

A moment was all it took. It flowed through him without interference in the same way that blood does. *Sean*, he thought. With that single name in his head, he made haste and strode down the stairs, removing his coat from the rack as he passed to the front door. He opened it with a sole purpose before him. Consumed, someone would have to pay for this. *Find Sean.*

*

For the first time in her life Jodie couldn't find the right words. She didn't want to explain the inexplicable but she'd been backed

141

into a corner. Something had to come out, but not the whole truth.

"Who did this to you?"

With her head held high Jodie said, "Sean."

A simple answer; the beginning of *her* truth.

"Sean?" her mother repeated, as though she'd heard the wrong answer.

"Sean." Jodie nodded. She smiled to try to diffuse the tension.

"Why? I mean, how?"

The questions made Jodie's head spin. Her heartbeat quickened, her skin crawled and her throat dried up. Her confidence abandoned her.

She decided to play on the wounds. Maybe she'd be able to save herself, at least. The threat and fear of her father on the other side of the bedroom door meant she had to do something. Her mother, she could manipulate; her father, no chance.

As her mother looked on, Jodie said, "Sean hurt me."

"But…" A pause as a nervous titter came out. "But that's ridiculous. Why would he do that?"

"Because…" It was Jodie's turn to pause, the words tugging back on her vocal cords.

"Why?" her mother implored, her voice far more urgent now.

"He's sick. You knew that when we brought him home."

"But something must have triggered him off."

As her mother opened her mouth to protest against the silence, the thought came to Jodie. *Let the manipulation begin.*

"Because he wanted to sleep with me."

A raised eyebrow – did her mother not believe her?

More. Give her more.

"And I said no."

"He what?" A fury charged through the small woman's voice and developed behind her eyes.

Now was the time to go for it. "He squeezed my throat and threw me down the stairs. Mum, he tore my skin."

"He did what?"

142

"He grabbed me by the hair and hit me."

Jodie had never seen such a display of anger in her mother, usually such an amiable woman. From her father, yes, several times, but never from her mother.

"In God's name we have to find him."

Had she pushed it too far? Her mother was behaving like a woman possessed.

"Where is he?" she scowled, taking her daughter by the shoulders. "We have to stop him."

Jodie sat dumbstruck, unable to respond, unable to think of how to turn this back to her advantage.

"Wake up!" Mrs Anderson roared. She snapped her fingers before Jodie's eyes, grabbing her attention. "We'll call the police. They'll find him. Attempted rape, the little bastard. We'll get you to the hospital. Then we'll track him down. He'll pay for this." Jodie's head shook a big *no* all the while her mother spoke.

Still shaking her head, Jodie resisted. "Mum, please, the police?" She felt a new kind of fear now; fear of the full truth revealing itself. "Listen, Mum, he's not all bad."

"What he did to you was sick. He needs to be punished. You remember he's got a past?"

Jodie knew she had to prevent her mother from going further. "And what if I wasn't completely innocent?" she asked, nervously. Her mother's head flicked in her direction. "You can't call the police. Dad can't know about everything that happened."

"Your father will make that boy sorry for the day he was born. I'll call the newspaper."

"No, no," Jodie jumped in. "You can't. Just listen, please. I'll tell you it all, just like it happened. But you've got to promise me we'll make it go away this once without Dad or the paper, or anyone else knowing anything."

"What are you saying? Why?"

"I'm asking you to let it go this time. He won't be back. That's obvious."

"But a young boy like that can't get away with something so-"

"He's not a young boy, Mum. And I'm not a young girl. That's the problem. Just leave it. Please."

"If the devil himself had done this I wouldn't-"

"I've slept with him before, okay?"

Mrs Anderson's body bent forwards like a fist had just knocked the wind right out of her and her mouth gaped wide open.

"I slept with him." Whether it was really meant or not, after a pause: "I'm sorry." She placed her head in her hand. Her gold rings pressed into her forehead.

After a few moments, Mrs Anderson inhaled deeply and managed to regain her strength. "Right," she murmured. But that was all she said.

Another pause.

Jodie could stand the silence no longer. "I'm no angel. You must know that."

"You can't tell Dad. I'm begging you."

"Of course I'm not going to tell your father," she snapped. "Do you think I'm mad? I don't know what I'm going to tell him, but certainly not the truth. He'd kill you. Forget about Sean. I mean, he'd do nothing but kill you if he found out." She seemed to lose sight of her daughter as she spoke. Her eyes focused beyond the child in need of help to a point next to her, and she saw only a blank wall. "Imagine the humiliation if this ever came out. If other people ever found out. What they'd say."

And, out of the blue, she snapped out of it. Her eyes locked on Jodie's. She saw the complete picture now. "So I think Sean didn't fit in here any more." The daughter shivered as she saw the intensity in the mother's eyes. "If anyone asks, Sean was put with a new family. That's right. He still had his troubles fitting in. All kids like him do. Ask anybody and they'll tell you that kids like him never change. They're trouble from the day they're born till the day we're fortunate enough to bury them in the ground. So we tried, but we couldn't make it work, just like everyone else whose lives that boy has tainted. And if he ever

144

comes back, well then, God help him because you've got no idea what will happen."

"Mum."

Mrs Anderson's mind was only with herself and she wouldn't listen to her daughter any more. Her gaze glided back to the pink wall and she remarked, "It didn't work out, Jodie."

Ignoring all else, Cassandra Anderson rose. She said, "What you've done."

She backed out of the room, leaving Jodie behind.

"Mum." An empty word, one that would no longer garner a response.

*

Jeff Anderson drove. Main roads, side streets and back alleys. Places you'd only associate with people like Mary Monroe. His eyes scanned everywhere. He peered through the rain drops as they mounted the windscreen and were brushed aside by the squeaky windscreen wipers.

He was looking for Sean, yet he was calm and restrained.

He imagined the conversation they'd have if he caught up with Sean, one which would have surprised his wife and daughter. He wouldn't just lunge in with fists flying, no matter how much his instincts told him to.

You're going to leave and never come back, he'd say to Sean. *You've got this one chance. Then I won't care any more and I'll tear you apart. And if that happens you and I will never be the same again.*

Sean would be surprised by this self-control, much like Anderson's own family would be. Sean would question why he'd be spared the beating.

Because I'm a man. I've seen you two together. I can read the body language. She plays with you and you let her. You both deserve what you get. I can see it, but my wife can't. She doesn't understand what you're like; in her goodness, maybe her naivety, she doesn't believe in your past. But I do. See, Sean, you and me, we're very much the same. I can see it in your eyes.

145

When I look into those bloodhound eyes of yours, I can see the things you've done. They never leave you. I saw a whirling rage behind your eyes the day I met you and I realised your potential. One day you're going to explode. Today was just the tip of the iceberg. I see your future and it's bleak, Sean. Because when you explode, there won't be a soul around to stop, help or protect you.

I don't let on, but I know a lot more about Jodie than she thinks I do. I watch. And I've watched you together. The times you're together, I see it in your eyes; you look at her and you want to fuck her. And she wants you to think that. It's merely part of her game. Fucking with us all. Even so, she can't protect herself. So that's where I come in. Because she's my daughter. No matter what she does, I'll protect her. Which is why I'm telling you to get the fuck out.

And then the next guy, I'll speak to him and he'll leave too.

My wife and daughter, they think I'm a monster. I have a temper, but what they fail to see is that I can control it. I use it only when it's necessary. My goal is always simple: keep my family safe from danger, and I will. Right now, you are that danger and God only knows what you could be in the future. Maybe she deserved it. So? Who gives a shit? My family is not going to be fucked over and fucked up by this, so you keep your mouth shut, disappear, and no one else will get hurt. You got that?

That's precisely how it would have been delivered, and Sean would have listened, and he would have followed instructions.

But the drive bore no fruit, so Jeff Anderson resigned and saved his battle for another time.

He headed for home.

146

Tomorrow

We awoke early the next morning and got a taxi to the train station. We had with us Sarah's suitcase and a duffel bag into which I'd managed to fit all my belongings.

I'd booked a hotel at which Sarah would stay while I visited the Andersons. I thought going alone was best, even though I craved her by my side to help me. The hotel would be our first stop.

The journey was pleasant, except the thoughts of what was to come preyed on me. We passed a lot of woodland, much of which I was sure I'd seen before.

Sarah and I continued to talk but about trivial things – the first time we hadn't been in deep conversation since our first night together.

I had no idea about what kind of reactions my arrival would provoke when I knocked on that door. Hostility, I hoped to avoid, but with Jeff Anderson it was highly unlikely.

I went in the hotel with Sarah when we arrived and helped her settle in. With the shirt I'd brought unpacked, I cleaned up and dressed. A pale green polo shirt was my choice along with a pair of beige trousers. I hoped I looked right. One kiss, a final kiss, gave me a modicum of hope; Sarah gave me strength.

The elevator ride back down to the lobby seemed to take an age. If I ever prayed, now would be the time. I thought they'd probably just close the door in my face and be done with it. Even though I wanted to do the right thing and apologise, I also wanted a future with Sarah, so success with the Andersons, for whatever reason, was necessary.

I had a taxi driver drop me off a couple of streets away from the Andersons' home. I needed extra time to think. What would my opening line be? Did I need an opening line? I was so confused.

Fairly soon I turned into the street I'd once called home. As the familiar sight stood before me, several memories of my past life flooded over me. How the family welcomed me and helped me settle down and got me through the early stages; how we developed a kind of bond and I became one of the family, like the son they never had, and a brother; but then a lover, and how a return to my old ways was only a stone's throw away; how I finally ran from this street with nothing but the clothes on my back and left destruction behind.

I walked along the footpath. The familiar sight of flowers had disappeared. I knocked on the door. The paint had begun to chip away. I cleared my throat. Who would answer? Mr Anderson's car wasn't in the driveway, but he may have used the garage. Maybe no one was home. *What will I do then?* I thought. Maybe feel relieved.

The door creaked on its hinges as it opened. The inside of the house revealed itself to me. And before it, the face of Mr Anderson.

I didn't say a word.

"Sean." Surprise. "What are you doing here? We've been looking for you."

Behind the shock, a slight smile fed into his cheekbones. But I didn't think he was pleased to see me.

The most important words were ready to come out. I said simply, "I'm sorry. Really, I am."

"Perhaps you should come in."

I had to make right the wrong. That would mean seeing Jodie. They deserved that much.

I followed Mr Anderson into the lounge area where we'd shared many happy hours as a family. Since I'd left, had there been any more?

"Is Mrs Anderson home?" I asked.

"Oh, she'll be back shortly. She's gone food shopping. The cupboards are empty." Unusual, for she'd always shopped well in advance. "Take a seat."

148

The furniture had been rearranged since I'd last been there. I chose one of the sunken green armchairs. My body disappeared into it.

"What about Jodie?" I asked. "Is she here?"

"No, she's out. Besides, I'm not sure if it's a good idea you two see each other. Of course, it'll be down to her to decide. I'm expecting her any minute too."

If Jodie allowed it I'd do whatever I could to make it up to her, if that were ever possible.

Mr Anderson and I looked at each other for a time without saying anything. Whenever he fixed his eyes on me, I got the impression that he was trying to stare me out or size me up or read my thoughts, but his pleasant-enough welcome indicated otherwise. Behind those eyes I began to realise he obviously knew everything about what had happened between his daughter and me. I wondered how that would make a father feel and I considered asking him, but my better judgement stopped me.

"Mr Anderson, I'd just like to-"

"Just tell me one thing, Sean. You ran away why? You knew we cared about you, yet you ran without a word. Sure, you fucked up quite badly, but we could've found a way through it. That's what families do. They work things out."

Maybe after some months' thought, he saw this. Or had he truly changed? "All I can say is I'm sorry," I said, "and I really have no answer for you. I didn't know what I was doing. It seemed like the best thing to do at the time."

"We always hoped you'd come back." Still something was lurking behind his eyes but I couldn't work out what. "We even kept your stuff and Cassandra makes up your room as she did before."

"What about Jodie? I hurt her."

"I know." He seemed non-committal. "That shouldn't have happened. Sure, she was annoyed with you – probably still is." He finally sat down opposite me. He chose the comfortable sofa, normally his wife's favourite place. "But wounds, Sean, they heal."

He leaned forwards, his elbows on his knees. "The thing is – and it's taken me a while to see this – Jodie was a confused girl. Weak too. The attention she used to get was a way to counter her low self-esteem. She understands now that what she did with you was wrong. I've made sure she understands." He cupped his hands together. "You know, sometimes the only way is the hard way. She sees the errors of her ways now. And maybe she won't be very pleased to see you, but she'll realise that what's happened is in the past and it's over. I want it that way. So do you or you wouldn't have come back."

He'd surprised me. The threats and anger I'd expected failed to appear. We were actually having a conversation. But his eyes wouldn't let me relax just yet.

"Where have you been staying?" he asked.

I drew a verbal map of my home. Then I went for it: "I've met a girl. Sarah. I've been staying with her brother. He gave me some work."

"Oh, what kind of work?"

I hadn't forethought this.

"Her brother has a small business. I help him out. And he helps me out."

"And this Sarah. What's she like?"

The jump of topic surprised me. I was still thinking about how to elaborate on Jimmy's business.

"Sarah? She's amazing. With her it's like I'm experiencing something I never want to let go."

He nodded his head. "Good. But sorry to tell you this. That feeling wears out. It's sad but true. Time's all it takes."

I ignored him, even though I wanted to tell him he was wrong. I had to use this moment to mention the States.

"She's only visiting. She lives in America. I've decided to go back with her."

"Go with her?" The pitch of his voice rose.

"We want to be together."

"Ah, that's right. Love. I'd forgotten. It can make you do foolish things."

"It's not foolish. We're happy together."

150

"Relationships, Sean, you can't believe they all work out. It doesn't happen. You like someone, you think you fall in love, and then you *actually* fall in love. Then after the initial excitement wears off you fall out of love. You can even hate them, Sean. Then something happens and, for a day, two days, three days, however long, you think you love again. It's like cheap paint, love. It doesn't stay there for long. Then you apply another layer. On and off. That's a relationship. Before you know it, it's too late to do anything about it and you're stuck."

"I won't be stuck. I'll be with Sarah, where I want to be. Away from the past. I want to live for the future."

"We all have pasts we want to forget, Sean. They don't go away so easily. All that stuff that's happened in your life leaves its mark. You can't just forget about your life. Believe me, I know." He thought for a moment. "Or was it all her? Did she really tell us the truth?"

"I was wrong. It was me." I pronounced each word crisply. "I should've been punished."

"There's still time," he sniggered. Then he continued as if he'd said nothing. "No, you've already been punished, Sean." He sunk into the sofa. "Now you have to enjoy life. If there's one thing I know, you never know when it'll be taken away from you. Life's too short. You've been through a tough time, but it's over now."

"I can't forget what I did. I can't forgive myself."

"All those things are in your past. The past can either burn or be burned, Sean. It's up to you to decide which. We'll all be punished one day, Sean. Where, when or how, we won't know, but it'll come. So until then, enjoy."

His calmness shook me. What was there behind his eyes?

"All I need is the chance to prove my love to Sarah and everyone will see how much I've changed."

"I believe it."

With that he nodded and made his way out of the room.

"Drink?" he asked as he left.

*

We were still settled on the sofa and chair with a couple of Cokes before us. He'd even brought out a few snacks for while we waited.

"What about your mother, Sean?" he asked. That got my attention. "Do you know where she is?"

"No."

I didn't know anything about her and kept my head down, staring at the bubbles in my glass. "Do you?"

"When we took you in, they told us she'd be moving far away. Some kind of rehab. And that we'd never hear from her again." He paused. "How do you feel about your mother?"

"How can I feel?" I said. "Your mother abandons you. You tell me."

"Maybe she didn't fight for you because she wanted a better life for you."

"Or maybe she was stoned," I said with too much hostility in my voice.

"It took some time to find you a new home where you could settle down. I know that. But you found it here with us. We proved everyone wrong. But a child always has a special bond with a parent, no matter what. Even if they don't speak. It's something you can't fully understand until you have a child of your own. I'm sure she feels that way, Sean. Does that change anything?"

"I don't know her. I don't want to. I guess I just feel anger."

"Of course." He nodded and sipped his drink. "Would you ever think about meeting your mother after all this time? To see what kind of person she is now?"

I didn't answer him. There was no possible answer to that.

"Sean?"

"When I was with her," I began after some thought, "I remember crying. Feeling miserable. I remember being scared, always worrying about how the next guy she'd bring through the door would treat me. No child should see their mother like that. You see that, you become something bad."

152

"That may well be true, but you don't feel that mother-child bond?"

"No," I answered plainly.

"It must be there. You love her?"

"No."

"You loved her?"

"No. I was too young. I don't know what I felt."

"You care for her?"

"I don't know her." His questioning was frustrating me. "Why do you keep talking about her anyway? I don't understand."

"I recently met your mother, Sean."

I sat there motionless.

"I have a number."

My mother. It had been eight years. Since she'd abandoned me. I wondered what I'd say if we ever met. Did she know the pain she'd caused? Did she know what had become of me? Would I dare tell her?

I settled on it. "I can't see her. We don't belong together any more."

"She's cleaned up, Sean," he said, rather over eagerly. "She's clean and she's turning her life around. I know a phone call from you would make all the difference to her."

"Why ask me?"

"She told me. She came looking for you."

I shook my head. "I don't know." I didn't want to, especially now when I just wanted to leave England behind, start fresh in America. "I need time. Don't make me decide now."

"It's here, Sean." He patted his breast pocket. "If you want it then it's no problem. Just say the word."

*

"What's Jodie up to anyway?" I asked.

The conversation had finally shifted topic. This was something I wanted to know far more than anything else.

"She's still studying," he said. "She's more careful now with everything she does. After you left, it was like a wake-up call to her – we all needed one really. She's a good kid now. Does as she's told, helps out around here, tries hard. She's trying to look after herself, grow up, mature. Everyone should worry about themselves and be their own top priority, so long as they have care for others at the same time. I hope you've learned that too." I nodded. "She knows she's made a lot of mistakes. But they're in her past now. Just like yours should be. It's only sad that some mistakes live with us longer than others." He stood up and walked over to the window. "What you've got to remember about families, Sean, and it's also what you forgot the day you left, is that they support each other. No matter what difficulty they face, they pull through. Take your mother, for instance." We were back on this again. "Even though she's had problems she's somehow managed for eight years. That's got to count for something."

I swallowed the remainder of my drink, unwilling to return to discussing someone who was nothing more than a stranger to me.

"I'll get you another," he said, moving over to take my glass from me.

Before he'd reached my glass we heard the lock in the door being tried. Mrs Anderson, slightly greyer now, stepped into view with three shopping bags wrapped around her fingers. The pained expression she had from carrying them quickly changed, developed into something far worse, and she froze.

"Hello, Mrs Anderson," I said by way of reintroduction.

"Sean."

As Mr Anderson faced his wife, I attempted to engage her in conversation for a second time. "It's nice to see you."

With the pace of a sluggish creature she came towards me, dropping the bags to the ground. What I got as she came face to face with me was a slap on the cheek. She spat her words out. "How could you come here after all this time, after what you did, just when we've got over you, and expect everything to be jolly, like nothing happened?"

154

"Honey," Mr Anderson said, "calm down. Sean's come here to apologise."

"After what he did to Jodie, how could you?"

I blushed further. I wanted to be out of there. I wanted to run again and hide. I'd expected hostility earlier and not got it from Mr Anderson. That had made me relax. Now with my guard down the docile wife's attack was far more devastating.

Mr Anderson helped me out again. "Honey, we discussed this before, remember? What would we do if Sean returned, if he came back to us? Now act just like we agreed." He took his wife aside and whispered to her but still within earshot of me. "I told you, everything will work out. Just treat him as you've always done." He turned back to me and winked. Coming over to me and pressing his hand on my shoulder, he said, "You can't expect her not to be angry with you. Remember that when Jodie comes home because she might take it even worse. It just takes time."

"I hope-"

"I've had a long time to think and I've done a lot of thinking. They'll be like me one day."

I noticed that Mrs Anderson had left the room. I could hear noises in the kitchen.

"We are all better than that," he added. "We are."

Mrs Anderson returned to the room after a few minutes.

"I came back to apologise, Mrs Anderson. I've learned a lot while I've been away and I want you to know how sorry I am." I looked on hopefully, expectantly, hopelessly. "I know I did wrong, but I've really changed so much."

Her raspy voice engaged. "You seem to forget all too easily what you did when you were younger. You hurt my daughter."

"Now, now honey. We both know it was a two-way thing," Mr Anderson said.

"She's my daughter."

"Honey-"

"She's *our* daughter, Jeff! No one, no matter who they are or what they've done, deserves to be subject to that."

"And I suppose the abuse you're dishing out to Sean now is acceptable then?"

I seized the moment. "If I'm not mistaken, you were going to call for help with the shopping, weren't you?"

"Oh, yes," she said.

"Allow me," I said, and I made a welcomed exit.

The fresh air was truly refreshing. After unloading the car's boot, I carried the bags into the kitchen, unpacked the shopping and put everything where it belonged – nothing had changed. Mrs Anderson, always by my side, thanked me.

"My pleasure," I answered. "I still remember all those times we went shopping."

"I suppose change can be positive," she said to her husband. He nodded in response to her and smiled, that same smile. "Go and settle back in the lounge, Sean. I'll prepare some fresh snacks. We can catch up."

I obeyed her and walked into the hallway. As soon as I left the room and closed the door behind me, muffled conversation erupted between husband and wife.

The carpeted floor remained fluffy as ever. Pictures hung on the wallpaper; even one of me remained, the whole family surrounding me on a sunny day. Mr and Mrs Anderson, Jodie still radiant, and me before any of the troubles began, unsure and ignorant of what was to come. All the smiles in the photograph were genuine – happy to be together.

I came to the living room and sat down again. The three-piece suite was immaculately maintained. There was an elegant wooden border that surrounded the room, separating two shades of wallpaper: the top was white and patterned with flowers and the bottom, a light shade of green. More pictures were carefully placed on the walls. A lampshade stood in the closest corner of the room. Speakers that connected to the television and stereo were placed for the best amplification possible. The dining room was connected to the living room. Near the far back wall and well out of the way stood the dining table, alone and unwelcoming, the opposite of the homely lounge. However out of place the table looked, though, it never lost its lustre. Today it remained shiny as ever.

I walked over to the back window. The curtains were still drawn, so I opened them. I almost stepped back from the surprise. The back garden, once so promising and full of beauty, had transformed into a patch of dry yellow grass and cracked, dirty cobble stones. Days when the garden was one of the finest in the neighbourhood and open for all to see flooded back to me. I couldn't understand the change. A high fence had been erected and suddenly this one-time public place had been hidden from everyone.

Mrs Anderson came into view as I returned to my seat. She was carrying a tray of drinks and three varieties of cake, along with blue-patterned plates that she'd bought in Venice. Mr Anderson followed behind, a rather awkward sight, carrying more snacks and a salad. They set the trays down on the coffee table and Mrs Anderson passed the plates and cutlery around.

"Thank you," I said.

"Help yourself," she said. She looked pleased with herself. "So Jeff tells me you've got yourself a lady friend."

"Yes," I said. "Her name's Sarah. We're very close, even though we haven't known each other for long."

"Oh, how long?"

"I met her this week." They both snorted a laugh. I felt disgusted and put the cake I'd selected down. I carried on defiantly. "Everything's perfect. We're going to make it last. I'm going to America with her."

"Yes," she said, dismissively. "Jeff mentioned something about that fancy."

"It's not a fancy. It's important." I stopped. I was cut off by the sound of the front door opening.

"I wish you luck," said Mr Anderson.

"I'm home," a voice called before Jodie came into view.

"Sweetheart," Mrs Anderson said, and she went to the corridor.

Jodie looked over her mother's shoulder at me. A weak smile appeared on her face, but no words came. I could see, even

157

from a distance and without properly meeting her, she'd changed a lot. The sexy tight outfits had been replaced by grey jeans, a white T-shirt and a black jacket. The make-up once painted on so thickly had vanished. She mouthed my name, but nothing was audible. I felt like I'd once again breached her security and I felt wrong.

"Hello Jodie," I said. "How are you?" A lame introduction, but I didn't know how to start.

She mustered up the words, "Not bad." I saw her swallow. "You're well?"

"Quite good. Thanks."

"Wow." Her body relaxed. "This is harder than I thought it would be." She nodded her head and said, "Give me a moment, would you?"

With that she turned and went up the staircase.

"Don't worry, Sean," Mr Anderson encouraged. "What did you expect from her anyway?" He laughed, but to and for himself. "You couldn't have fooled yourself that it would be that easy."

"At least she wasn't angry."

Mrs Anderson returned some moments later. I didn't know she'd been upstairs to check on Jodie. "She's ready to see you."

Mr Anderson's eyebrows lowered, but he gave me a consenting nod.

I made my way to the room I'd last been in on the night of our fight. This is where it all began. The first time, the drunken climb up the stairs and leading Jodie back to her room, unaware of what would follow a week later. The start of the brief affair, which resulted in a fist fight, torn flesh and lives forever altered. I recalled the pain of the fall as I stared at the carpet, the bloodstains removed but the memories always there.

I'm different now.

Without a clue about how to begin I knocked on the door and opened it after Jodie asked me to enter. I put my smile on and showed my face around the door.

"Hi," I said.

"Hi," she said. "Come in."

I entered and sat on the swivel chair.

"Before anything," I started, "I want to say I'm different now. Please don't be worried about my being here."

"I can see that, Sean. I can see it in your eyes."

"You look great. And for the problems I've caused, it may not be enough, but I'll always be sorry."

"I understand." Then she surprised me. "And I'm sorry too."

I asked, "So what have you been up to?"

"Everything's new for me. Mostly I've been catching up with my studies. I want to do well."

"Good for you," I said.

"And you? What are you doing?"

"Oh, so much. Too much, really. I'm preparing to go to America. I've met someone and I want to be with her."

"Girlfriend?"

I nodded and my grin returned.

"I worked with her brother and she's over, but she's going back. I want to go with her. You know, your parents keep sending me these mixed signals."

"They've always been like that. Nothing's ever clear with them. You must remember that."

"Yeah, but what if they won't give me my passport back? I need it to go."

"They will," she said. "Or I will."

"Thank you, Jodie."

"You love her, don't you?"

"Very much."

"I can see it in your eyes," she repeated.

"It's real."

"So don't worry," she said, leaning forwards, tapping me on the elbow. "They won't stand in the way of true love. I won't let them."

"What about you?" I asked. "Boyfriend?"

"Oh, no, not at the moment. Not since you left. They're pretty careful about what they let me do. I haven't mentioned it to them yet, but I really want to get a job. Get some of my independence back."

"You look really good. The new look suits you. And your hair too."

"Thanks. It's growing on me. So long as I'm different on the outside, you know?" For the first time, there was some regret in her voice.

She put her head down. "They changed me. I wanted to, sure, but not everything. Yes I'm better and I want to be, but I don't feel like me any more."

"But Jodie-"

"That day changed me, Sean. And it also changed you. But it changed my parents too. They became so controlling. They took my life away."

Suddenly, *sorry* seemed an inadequate word.

"It'll be fine," I said.

I saw in her eyes that she didn't believe me, but she was thankful for my company.

"I know," she said.

*

I left over an hour later with an invitation to return for supper with Sarah that evening. I accepted.

I walked towards the town centre to catch a taxi. They'd offered me a lift, but I wanted some time to take it all in. As I walked, I thought about Sarah and how lucky I was to have found her. All around me, I saw couples and I felt at home.

I returned to the hotel where I found Sarah watching television. I told her of our invitation and filled her in on my time with the Andersons while we got ready to head out. Although clearly nervous about going, she realised the importance of having a successful second visit. The page, she said, had almost been wiped clean, and it was time to start over.

Could I have wanted anything more? Could I have expected anything less?

Before Today

Within three days of being on the streets again, I met the wrong crowd.

Within two weeks I had my first fix again. My battery felt recharged. I felt like I'd lost.

Within a month I was open for business again.

Every morning I went to sleep, crumbling. Every night I woke up, got high and worked without knowing I was doing it. The women left me alone this time. The guys, though, they still hit and bit. Harder than before. But the drugs soothed the pain.

I shared a flat with another woman. She always talked about working from home. I'd never thought about it. I thought it could be a way to control the bruises and black eyes. Select the clients more maybe.

Within a year I was pregnant. I didn't know my son. I lost him the day I gave birth to him. Every day, I filled myself up with drugs. He was around, but I didn't see him. I didn't play with him. I didn't do the mummy thing. And I didn't notice the day they took him from me. I can't even tell you how long it was before I found out. But the day I did I sunk into a crater I couldn't leave. I'd ruined my son's life.

Nothing makes you sober quicker. I turned myself back in and pleaded to start over.

Evening

We arrived at the Andersons', again by taxi and then on foot, hopeful that what was to come would be special. All the while, I showed Sarah places behind which there were stories.

Looking at the house, we stepped onto the doorstep. Sarah looked pleased to be here, yet I was uneasy. She reassured me that everything would be all right.

Mr Anderson answered the door. As the door opened, I caught a glimpse of his unusual smile. It quickly disappeared. "Ah," he said. "Welcome, welcome." He made sight of Sarah and added, "And you must be the lovely Sarah. I've heard a lot about you. Do come in."

"Thank you," she answered, and took his hand as we stepped in.

When we were standing at the bottom of the staircase, he said, "Let me take your coats." We gave them to him and were told, "Go through."

I winked at Sarah and led her with an arm around her waist into the lounge. There I came to a halt like a truck had just crossed my path. Sarah grabbed hold of me, sensing that something was wrong.

I stood motionless. Our eyes met. They were dark eyes. Nervous eyes. In a beige jacket and trousers she stood there. Behind the sofa, a glass of orange juice in her hand, and barely recognisable to me after so many years, but I instantly knew who she was. She didn't move or make a sound. She just waited for my reaction. We hadn't seen each other for almost half my lifetime, but there she was and I knew.

A son always knows his mother, even if he doesn't know her.

All eyes were on me. Sarah remained by my side, her head turned towards mine. I said nothing. A strange sensation ran through my body. I can't describe it to this day.

Her hair was long and dark. A smile came across her face. She was taller than I remembered and looked older than I thought she would. Her face was filled with lines and a deeper than deep darkness sat below her eyes.

"Hello Sean."

Mr Anderson spoke up. "Surprise," he said, rather too enthusiastically.

She looked at me in anticipation. I could hear Mr Anderson biting his tongue and breathing heavily, yet still I remained silent. How do you begin a conversation with someone you've not seen for so many years? Or with someone you blamed every dark part of your history for? I was seventeen years old with no answer. I took a step back and began to shake my head. I felt Sarah's grip of my arm tighten and she whispered, "Steady."

She abandoned me.

Mr Anderson feebly repeated, "Surprise, Sean."

They deceived me.

Sarah said louder this time, "Be strong."

I wanted to break out of the room and cry freedom.

Unexpectedly, and as if to block the exit, she said, "Let me break the ice then. Sean, please know how difficult this is for me. I want to do right by you. I know it may be too little too late, but I owe you that much."

"And a lot more," I corrected her, coldly.

"I'm sorry."

"And you must be Sarah," Mrs Anderson said, heading for Sarah, arm outstretched.

"Right." Sarah held out her hand in return. "Nice to meet you."

"My husband, you just met," she added, pointing behind her. "And this is Sean's mother," she said, indicating the fifth person in the room.

My mother – I couldn't call her this back then – came towards us and said, "It's a pleasure."

She kissed Sarah on both cheeks and stood opposite me. I tried to look straight through her but noticed every detail on her face. Lines and the tiredness. She pressed the upper part of both my arms, causing Sarah's grip of me to be released.

"You look good," she told me and smiled. "I'm already proud of you."

Little did she know.

She kissed me on the right cheek and paused, awaiting my reaction. She didn't get one, so she pressed her lips softly against my other cheek. Something inside me – something I couldn't understand – responded to her touch.

"You've been through so much," she said.

"That, I have."

"And now look at you." She signalled to Sarah. "See how well you're doing. See everything you've got." Tears built up in her eyes.

Mr Anderson came to us and took her away by the arm. "Maybe we should sit down," he said.

"At the table," his wife said. "Dinner's ready."

She left the room and Sarah and I followed Mr Anderson and my mother to the table. Jodie, Mr Anderson informed us, was out with friends. I was surprised. "Spontaneous, she is," Mr Anderson said.

Dinner was served and conversation picked up. Mr Anderson acted like a conjunction in a sentence by bringing us all together, filling in the mini silences and keeping the wine flowing.

About an hour in, my mother cleared her throat, put her glass of water down and said, "I don't want to change the mood, but there are a few things I'd like to say." I braced myself. "First, thank you both for inviting me here and giving me the opportunity to see my son again. And, hopefully, to change his life forever and for the better." Mr and Mrs Anderson toasted their glasses together. "And thank you Sean for giving me this chance." I had no idea how to respond, so I kept my eyes lowered. "When you were born, I had a life but I really had no life. Very quickly the drugs came and trapped me. There was no way out. You have to believe that. You start and your life's over. I was thirteen when it all went wrong. A child."

And that was when it really hit me. Thirteen.

"You were born into a life I couldn't control. My senses had been taken away from me by the drugs. But they also made it so that I didn't feel the pain. I was sixteen when I first went into a clinic. I was there for eight months. But I ran away. My head was so messed up, so stupidly I ran from the one place that was trying to help me, from the only people who could've saved me. After you were born, the time came round when we were found and they took you away from me. That was when I truly came to my senses and I wanted to fight. I served time, then a clinic again. You can beat it, they tell you. We can beat it. *You* can beat it. And you know what? They're right. I did beat it." She cracked and dropped her head into her hand. She tried to hide the tears. Mrs Anderson, who was sitting to her side, tapped her arm softly.

"Why are you telling me these things?" I asked.

"Because I want you to understand. I know I ruined your childhood and I want to make it up to you."

"I've already made myself better."

"But a mother's love," she said. "I know what I'm speaking about. I never had a thing from my mother. Don't make me be like her. I beg you, Sean. I beat the drugs. Let me add something to your life and we'll both win, now before it's too late."

"You're asking a lot of me." I caught sight of Sarah's surprised expression. I told her, "What do you want me to say?"

"This is your mother, Sean. You've lost so much in your life. Now it's time to get something back."

"She's right," Mr Anderson concurred.

My mother continued. "They caught me soon after I ran. They caught me and locked me up for two years. I got worse, much worse, before I got better. It was hard, but look at me now. Here I am today with you. If you'd told me five years ago that

165

this was going to happen I wouldn't have believed it. I deserve a moment's happiness."

We all deserve hope; I was granted it.

Maybe she was right. Maybe it was time for it to be over. If I hadn't had a chance where would I be? *Where will she be if she isn't given the chance?*

"Spend tomorrow with me?" she asked. "Both of you. That's all I ask. If you don't ever want to see me again after that, so be it."

A second chance.

"Agreed," I said.

*

She'd managed to be clean of alcohol and drugs for about two years.

Early the next morning, Sarah and I got onto a train and made the thirty-minute journey to where we would meet my mother. She met us at the train station and picked us up by car. She'd been working in a supermarket, attempting to straighten out every aspect of her life. I guess I was the final aspect.

After about five minutes of driving and small talk, we got out of the car. A vast field of monuments stood before us.

"There's something here I want to show you," she said.

She wore a navy-blue suit, a white shirt, and looked elegant. We made our way to one of the plaques in the centre of the field. It was made of beige stone and had on it bold black writing. Red flowers surrounded the area. The grass was cut short and the park was immaculately kept.

"The last great war," she said as we came to a stop and stood behind her. Sarah's arm was linked in mine. "You know, your great-grandfather died during this war. He was a pilot, Sean." She pointed to the plaque and I saw the name. Gordon Monroe. My relative. History. Family. "I've not taught you anything. I don't know much myself. But I remember a few old pictures from when I was at home and I remember two names. Gordon and Ethel Monroe. That's it. I couldn't teach you before

166

– about family, about life, about how a person should be – because I didn't know, but now, now Sean, everything I know I want share with you. Starting right here. I want to introduce you to your great-grandfather."

We stood looking at the plaque, without the murmur of a word. A great many had died fighting for our futures and chances. We have to take them and make the most of them while we have the chance.

Throughout the day she showed us her town, we window-shopped and we had lunch in an Italian restaurant. Finally, to conclude a peaceful day, she took us to a park in which there was a lake. We sat on a bench, all of us talking about times gone by and our hopes for the future. I told Mum about our plans for America. Happiness, she said, she wanted for us, no matter what or where.

We stared at the fountain in the middle of the lake. Greek Gods and Goddesses sprayed water.

After six hours, we were back at the train station, happy, and we said our goodbyes.

"You will keep in touch?"

"Definitely," I answered.

I hugged her and she kissed Sarah goodbye.

"You take good care of my son, you hear." Her lip quivered.

"You bet," Sarah answered.

"You're so similar." She smiled.

"We'll call you when we get there," I said, and we went on our way. We waved.

Sarah was a moon of happiness on the way back to the hotel. I was beaming too.

She told me, "I'm so proud of you. Even I feel satisfied and she's your mother."

"Yes," I said. "You're right. It was wonderful."

"You still want to come, don't you?" Sarah asked. "To America, I mean."

"I wouldn't miss it for the world. Nothing about how I feel and what I want to do has changed. Always know that."

167

She placed her hand on my thigh and squeezed it. I did likewise.

"I feel so good with you," I told her.

After a brief silence, Sarah took a deeper breath. She said, "Your mum will want to be part of your life now."

"That's a good thing."

"Yes, it is." She turned to me and frowned for a second. "But how will it be if you're in America? You lost your mother before when you really needed her. What about now?"

"Remember, I never really had a mother."

She shook her head. "But you've got her now. And I know you don't want to lose her." She looked away sadly. "It's a chance I'm taking away from you if you come with me."

I hushed her. "You're giving me a life. You're not taking anything away from me. I believe in her for the first time ever. But from here or from America, it makes no difference to me. We'll be together and we can see her. It's not the end of the world we're going to. It's just America." I stroked her hair. "We have all the time in the world, Sarah. And we'll always be happy."

"Promise me," she said. "Promise me we'll always be together, we'll always be happy."

"I promise. Promise me?"

She smiled. And she giggled. "I promise."

Night

We were back at the hotel. Our room was filled with two single beds that were pushed together to create the illusion of a double. The duvet was patterned with green, blue and yellow. Two portraits of flowers hung on the main walls. The paint beneath was peeling away.

It wasn't until we were getting into bed that I remembered: the initial reason for my visit. Rolling out of bed, I said, "The passport. I forgot it."

"It's okay," Sarah said. "We can head round there tomorrow on our way to the airport."

We'd decided to leave early and arrive at the airport to see what flights still had seat availability. If we had to we'd wait another day and stay at an airport hotel.

"Call them," she told me.

I sat on the side of the bed and picked up the telephone. I dialled the Andersons' number from memory. It barely rang once before it was picked up. I heard a rush of air as the receiver was dragged at pace from its holder.

"Hello," Jodie said, quickly. Her voice was muffled and her breathing unsteady.

"Jodie, it's Sean."

"Oh God. Sean," she sobbed.

I rose from the bed. Sarah sprang up at my sudden movement. Jodie kept sniffing, much as she did that awful time in our past. Goose bumps packed along my skin and my hairs stood on end.

"Are you all right, Jodie?"

Sarah said, "Sean?"

I shrugged my shoulders at her. She came to my side on her knees.

"Listen to me. He'll be here in a second. I'm sure of it. Mum and Dad are furious with me and now I know why. They sent me away earlier. Sean, I'm sorry. I didn't know. You've got to help me."

"How? How can I help you?" I said with heightened tones.

"No one-"

Loud sounds erupted then disappeared.

"What's going on?" Sarah asked. She pressed on my arm.

"Jodie," I called into the telephone. "Jodie." I heard a few noises, something falling over, and then slow footsteps. Again I tried, "Jodie."

A slight pause, then a voice came on the line. "Sean. It's Mr Anderson here."

"What's happening? Where's Jodie? Is she okay?"

"Oh, I doubt she'll ever be okay thanks to you, but then again, are we all okay?"

"I don't understand, Mr Anderson."

"Sean," Sarah repeated, but I couldn't answer her. I didn't understand what was happening.

"You ruined her life."

I froze. Pictures of our pleasant yesterday wrestled with what happened before. "What are you talking about?"

"My fucking daughter," he said. "Not this time." He laughed with a sinister cackle. "Punishment, Sean. I always warned her. You can't escape it."

The man was speaking in riddles.

"What's wrong?" Sarah said, this time louder.

"I don't know," I whispered.

"Oh," Mr Anderson said loudly, piercing my ear, "the fair Sarah. Don't go fucking her, you hear. Punishment, Sean. You can't hide from it."

"I'll be there soon. She'd better be all right when I get there."

"Be more..." He started coughing. Then he mumbled something incomprehensible. He was drunk. "Who knows what'll happen." And the line went dead.

I replaced the receiver, not knowing what to think. The man who'd raised me, whom I'd deceived, who'd welcomed me back – what was going on with him? My nerves began to fail me and I trembled. Sarah held me.

I replayed the conversation to her. I begged her to stay at the hotel when she told me she'd come too. I couldn't involve her in this any further. It was going to be over and I would end it if necessary.

I arrived at the Anderson household within an hour. Darkness surrounded the house. Bounding out of the taxi, I headed for the front door and pounded on it.

Minutes passed but my knocking didn't subside until finally the door was prised apart. Mrs Anderson's face appeared. "Sean."

Then, unexpectedly, she let the door open fully and stepped back.

"Where's Jodie?" I asked, impatiently.

"Upstairs. And she won't be coming down."

"You can't keep her locked up," I protested.

"Can't I?"

I stepped clear into the hallway and passed her.

"Where's your husband? Someone's got to explain what's going on."

She didn't answer me.

"Fine," I said, and I made for the stairs.

"No!" she hollered, and she leapt in front of me. "Stop!"

"Tell me where he is!" I yelled at her.

I started to push through her. She grabbed me by the arm and slapped me on the face. "You'll be sorry," she sneered. Her cheeks were red like she'd burst vessels.

"Let me see Jodie. I'm not the kind of person you want to piss off, lady."

I got past her and placed a foot on the bottom step. She grabbed me from behind. I turned forcefully and she plunged backwards as if lifted by the wind.

When I got three steps up, I heard a deep voice and Mr Anderson appeared at the top of the staircase. He said, "That'll be far enough, thank you."

He slowly stepped down. I backed off the steps I'd taken, but I kept my game face on. It felt unnatural.

When he reached the bottom, he brushed past me and went next to his wife who was on the floor. He helped her up with one arm but kept his gaze on me. He said, "You come into my home. You threaten my wife and my family. You expect me to let you do that?" He raised his voice. "I don't fucking think so!" I was in a confrontation again, one I'd not dreamed of being in.

"I want to see Jodie. Either you let me see that she's all right or I'll go and find her."

"You know, I'm not some screwable fifteen-year-old little girl you can fuck with. I'm warning you. I'll fuck you up."

Squirrel-like, his wife went back to her knees. At the sight of her face and the sound of his ugly words, I lost it. *Enough*, I thought. *Fuck this.*

Fuck this.

"And I'm warning you," I erupt. "Come near me and you'll see what I was."

I can't control myself; I have to see Jodie.

I make for the staircase again. Anderson lunges to block me. He grabs me on the back of the shoulder and wrestles the sides of my arms. He begins edging me towards the door. There's no way I'm being thrown out of here. No way. I answer him with a knee to his groin. Pain envelopes his face and he releases my arms. Again I connect, this time with a kick and he goes down.

His wife pushes off the ground. She charges at me and I hold up my hand to stop her tearing at my face.

"Don't even try it, you bitch," I growl. One push with my arms and she sinks back to the ground. Two pictures fall from their wall hooks.

I manage to get up the stairs in five strides. I barge into Jodie's room.

Empty.

I check each room. All empty.

As I'm hurrying back down, Anderson, who's back on his feet, meets me on the staircase. His shoulder collides with my stomach and I'm stunned. Winded, I double over like a folding chair, and he takes hold of my trousers, swings and releases, sending me headfirst down the final few steps. My jaw ricochets off a step and my shoulder knocks over the telephone table.

For no more than three seconds I'm motionless, but it feels like an hour. My mind spins. I remember lying on the floor in the nightclub, unable to help Sarah. Dizziness then too. It can't happen again.

"Motherfucker," I hear Anderson say, and that's my calling card. I come to.

He passes me and seems to be heading for the kitchen. I get up – too quickly; I see more stars – and wildly, without much of a clue of where I am, shoulder-tackle his left knee. He goes down like an eager whore.

I taste blood. Then I get up and stand over him as I hear his wife sobbing. Jodie's sobbing. He looks pathetic. Coiled up and hugging his knee. I kick him and, as he falls back, I sit on his chest, a knee on each side of his body. Without thought my fist collides with his cheek.

"Where is she, you prick?" I say, my blood spitting down on him.

"No," Mrs Anderson calls through her hysterics. "The shed. She's in the shed. Leave him. This stupid game of yours." I don't know who she said it to, but I look at her, caught. Something makes me smile and fear spreads across her face. I even scare myself. I stare at Anderson and see him like I've never seen him before. He's weak.

I stand up and say quietly, "You know who I am."

But did I? For a moment my eyes close. I'm about to kick the man again. Punch him. Something to punish him. Now the bald guy in the club: I see his face and prepare to kick. Anderson curls up even further.

Had I learned nothing? I'd fitted back into me of the past perfectly, too easily.

My leg stayed stretched back for the kick. To assault this man like never before. He deserved a beating. I wanted to hurt him like he'd hurt Jodie. Or maybe I just wanted to hurt.

As Mrs Anderson gasped and gargled, only silence filled the air. And I didn't do it. I stopped myself. But to this day I believe I was capable of doing it. Instead, I stepped over him and made my way into the kitchen and out the back door.

The shed door wouldn't open, so I kicked it twice. The door careered open. I toppled over slightly. Even with minimal light I saw Jodie. She was bound to a chair.

Crying, as I released the gag that was stuffed in her mouth, she explained, "My punishment. See?"

I started to untie her with ferocious haste. The knots in the rope were tight and rubbed against my fingers.

"Thank you," she said.

I hugged her and asked, "What are your parents on?"

"Rage."

I paused, confused again, then pulled the ropes free.

"Let's sort this out. For good."

I led her by the hand back into the house. We found Mr and Mrs Anderson sitting at their respective places in the lounge: he on the arm chair; she on the sofa. At first glance, they appeared content, like they were enjoying a cup of tea together.

"Cut this out," I said. My head ached and my heartbeat was still pounding.

Mrs Anderson looked at her husband. She sniffed and wiped away a tear. He snorted with laughter like a scheming teenager misbehaving at the back of a classroom.

"Cut what out?" she asked innocently, but I heard a quiver in her voice. She couldn't pretend as well as he could.

"Tell me."

"Tell you what?" she asked but her voice still shook.

"Tell me why you locked your daughter up in the shed. Why your husband threw me down the fucking stairs."

"Oh dear-"

"Tell me!" I shouted, louder than ever.

"Why-"

"If he wants to know," the man of the house finally spoke, interrupting his wife. "He has a right to know, after all." He scratched his nose and wiped away the sweat that had built up on his forehead. The twisted grin returned to his face. "But to your grave it goes, Mr Monroe."

No one has ever called me that.

"What does?"

"Dad?" Jodie said.

"The truth," he said. "It's time you knew."

*

"You see, Sean, I hold this over you. Against you I'll always win. I let you into my family. Despite what you were. And then you brought it in here."

"Brought what in here?"

"Your sickness. You didn't give a fuck. Who gives a fuck if you fuck my daughter? I do! Well now, my friend, *you* will give a fuck. You'll regret the days you've sinned."

Not for the first time I couldn't express myself amid the confusion. "What do you mean?" I eventually asked.

Very matter of fact, he started. "Your mother shot up once too often. The same needle that infected her infected her unborn child. You, Sean, you're dying. You have AIDS."

Stunned. A world fell apart. My world. My life.

I heard Jodie sob, but I couldn't react. I couldn't help her this time. Her mother's head fell down and she shrieked.

And I realised.

"Then…" but I couldn't even finish my sentence.

Allowing time for it to set in, Mr Anderson broke the silence. His wife still couldn't look up. "Think of all you've gained. Think of all you now love. And now think of all you're going to lose."

Sarah. Mum. Life.

Tears came but without sounds. My body trembled. Fear spread through me and I fell to my knees. Sarah had to be all right. Dying, I could live with, but causing the death of my love, no.

Jodie placed her arm around my shoulder, helped me to my feet and started to step backwards. I followed her lead.

Mrs Anderson was still sunk. Her husband hadn't noticed.

As we backed out, Anderson said, "Do you know what this is?"

"Punishment," the only word to escape my otherwise muted lips.

"Retribution," he corrected, shaking his head. "Your damnation."

Jodie spoke up. "And your punishment?" she said to her father. "Can you guess? You haven't got a daughter any more."

His eyes narrowed. We were almost out of the room, but I couldn't feel the movements we made.

"What are you talking about?" he said. "Look at what he's done," and he pointed at me.

"Goodbye," Jodie said. "You sad, pathetic man."

"No," he repeated. "No. What he's done to you. Did I have a choice?"

We were through the front door when I heard a loud scream. "Did I have a choice?"

Ahead

Jimmy got what was coming to him. He couldn't get away with what he was doing for ever. Allowed himself to believe the hype that followed him around. Made a danger of himself.

He could easily have been killed. Six weeks after our arrival in America it happened. They came to the house. The house in which Sarah and I felt so safe. The same three guys from the club and armed with knives. They came to kill Jimmy.

But Jimmy was ready. The window shattered downstairs. Jimmy, upstairs, heard. He prepared himself. They came to him. Quietly, they thought. They searched in each of the rooms, knives ready to strike. They checked the wrong door last.

Jimmy's door.

There he stood, gun in hand. That was Jimmy. Think you've got one up on him and he comes back ten times harder. Think a knife's enough and you stare a gun in the face.

He didn't hesitate. He fired three times. Two dead instantly. The other, hit in the neck, maimed for life. Those who came to Jimmy to maim, maimed.

The police arrived shortly after. Jimmy's parents arrived home from their dinner and dance just in time to see him being carted off in a police car. Just in time to decide to abandon him for good.

He'll be in prison for the rest of his life. Punished for his sins.

Me, I always knew one day I'd be punished. So many sins can't be ignored; Jimmy and I are both living proof of that.

No matter what my destiny is, though, I know that Sarah and Jodie won't die like me. Sarah crumbled at the news. It took her time to recover, but we love each other, and love is stronger than anything else. She's not infected and she'll help me. I'm going to die in love. What more can a person want?

After we left the Andersons behind for ever, Jodie slipped my passport into my back pocket. That gave me some comfort. She told me to go and enjoy every moment. So here we are, Sarah and me, in America, living our life together, trying to remain optimistic, trying to be unconscious of the future. We live for the now; every day is special and we live on, at peace with one another, despite the single thought that lurks quietly at the back of our minds: what will become of me. You see, death is a sad thing, selfish and selfless at the same time. It comes into our lives, takes hold and never lets us go, from the time we enter to the time we depart. I might feel the impact of death before others feel the impact of mine. We don't know, yet we don't live wanting to know. Sarah, my mother and I take each day as it comes and we appreciate each day for what it brings.

It always brings Sarah; she who changed my life, she who made me. I am Sarah, I love her and, wherever we are, we'll be together for all time.

You can judge me, judge what I did, judge what happened to me; judgement is fine. I won't point my finger at you and complain. Maybe I got what I deserved. But no matter what you think of me, believe me when I tell you one thing: I wouldn't have had it any other way.

Biography

After studying literature, linguistics and Spanish at university, Karl Vadaszffy trained as an English teacher and an actor. He has edited magazines, taught English as a foreign language and is currently the Head of English at a school in Hertfordshire. As a freelance journalist, his articles regularly appear in seven magazines that cover the automotive, aerospace, technology and travel industries. To find out more about Karl visit his website: www.karlvad.co.uk.

* Photograph taken by Karen Scott

Lightning Source UK Ltd.
Milton Keynes UK
11 November 2009

146092UK00001B/28/P

9 780956 373304